P9-CET-454

"We Have To Be Lovers."

"We what?" Gwen growled. "No way. That's so not part of the deal. We've been there and done that. It didn't work then—it sure as hell won't work now."

"My father's expecting to see a devoted couple."

Gwen froze. She had a very bad feeling. "How devoted?"

"We have to convince him it's a love match."

"I can't do it."

"Look, let's not forget what you get in all this. You're not doing it out of love." He'd dealt his trump card, and they both knew it. She'd do anything to keep her house. Anything. If that meant being Declan's radiant, devoted bride, she had to agree.

"Okay, I'll do it." Her voice was reduced to a whisper.

"We'd better get some practice in, then."

Dear Reader

When I was in primary school I met a girl who'd been "promised" to a young boy by her family. I remember being amazed that a marriage could be arranged when you were so young, and it was the fodder for many a daydream. Since then, I've always loved to read tales of arranged marriages and marriages of convenience, and I had a lot of fun writing this one, where I pushed together two people who really felt they ought to be apart.

The first version of this story won the Romance Writers of New Zealand 2004 Clendon Award. Back then Declan had a different name and was helping his brother out as a topless waiter when he met Gwen. The original idea came from my hairdresser who, together with a group of good friends, has ladies' days that are catered by...you guessed it...hunky male topless waiters. Of course, that part of the story has now gone, but the incendiary attraction between Declan and Gwen still burns, as does, I hope, your enthusiasm for the Knight brothers. Watch out next for Mason and Helena's story—available this March—for one more New Zealand Knight!

With very best wishes,

Yvonne Lindsay

THE CEO'S CONTRACT BRIDE

YVONNE LINDSAY

Silhouette
Desire

Published by Silhouette Books
America's Publisher of Contemporary Romance

If you purchased this book without a cover you should be aware that this book is stolen property. It was reported as "unsold and destroyed" to the publisher, and neither the author nor the publisher has received any payment for this "stripped book."

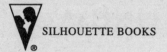 SILHOUETTE BOOKS

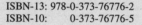

ISBN-13: 978-0-373-76776-2
ISBN-10: 0-373-76776-5

THE CEO'S CONTRACT BRIDE

Copyright © 2007 by Dolce Vita Trust

All rights reserved. Except for use in any review, the reproduction or utilization of this work in whole or in part in any form by any electronic, mechanical or other means, now known or hereafter invented, including xerography, photocopying and recording, or in any information storage or retrieval system, is forbidden without the written permission of the editorial office, Silhouette Books, 233 Broadway, New York, NY 10279 U.S.A.

All characters in this book have no existence outside the imagination of the author and have no relation whatsoever to anyone bearing the same name or names. They are not even distantly inspired by any individual known or unknown to the author, and all incidents are pure invention.

This edition published by arrangement with Harlequin Books S.A.

® and TM are trademarks of Harlequin Books S.A., used under license. Trademarks indicated with ® are registered in the United States Patent and Trademark Office, the Canadian Trade Marks Office and in other countries.

Visit Silhouette Books at www.eHarlequin.com

Printed in U.S.A.

Books by Yvonne Lindsay

Silhouette Desire

*The Boss's Christmas Seduction #1758
*The CEO's Contract Bride #1776

*New Zealand Knights

YVONNE LINDSAY

New Zealand born to Dutch immigrant parents, Yvonne Lindsay became an avid romance reader at the age of thirteen. Now, married to her "blind date" and with two surprisingly amenable teenagers, she remains a firm believer in the power of romance. Yvonne balances her days between a part-time legal management position and crafting the stories of her heart. In her spare time, when not writing, she can be found with her nose firmly in a book, reliving the power of love in all walks of life. She can be contacted via her Web site, www.yvonnelindsay.com.

With heartfelt thanks beyond words,
to my wonderful husband, children and family,
for all your support and encouragement
and for always standing by me
and believing in my dream.

One

"Six weeks until the tender closes, mate."

Declan Knight leaned back his office chair and grimaced at his youngest brother's words as they echoed down the telephone line. He shot an irritated glance at his Rolex—yeah, six weeks. He could count off the seconds he had left to find the finance he needed to pull this project off.

"Don't remind me," he growled.

"Hey, it isn't my fault Mum put that stipulation in her will for our trust funds. Besides, who'd have thought you'd still be one of New Zealand's most wanted bachelors?"

Declan remained silent. He sensed Connor's instant discomfort over the crackling line.

"Dec? I'm sorry, mate."

"Yeah, I know." Declan interrupted swiftly before his brother could say another word. "I gotta move on."

Move on from the reality that he hadn't been able to save Renata, his fiancée, when she'd needed him most. For a minute he allowed her face to swirl through his memory before fading away to where he kept the past locked down—locked down with his guilt.

"So, you want to go out tonight? Have a drink maybe? Show the Auckland nightspots how to have a really good time?" Connor's voice brought him back instantly.

"Sorry, previous engagement." Declan scowled into the mouthpiece.

"Well, don't sound so excited about it. What's the occasion?"

"Steve Crenshaw's prewedding party."

"You're kidding, right? Watch-the-paint-dry Steve?"

"I wish I were kidding." The pencil Declan had been twiddling through his fingers snapped—the two pieces falling unheeded to the floor. His staid and übercautious finance manager was marrying the one woman in the world who was a constant reminder of his failure, and his deepest betrayal—Renata's oldest and dearest friend, Gwen Jones.

"Maybe you should ask him for some tips on how to find a wife."

Declan's lips tweaked into a reluctant smile as he heard the suppressed laughter in his brother's voice. "I don't think so," he answered.

"You're probably right. Okay then. Don't do anything I wouldn't do. Ciao, bro'."

Declan slowly replaced the receiver. It wasn't that he was short of women, in fact the opposite was true, but he sure as hell didn't want to *marry* any of them. There wasn't a single one who wouldn't expect declarations of undying devotion—devotion he was incapable of giving.

He'd been there, done that. He would bear the scars forever. Losing Renata had been the hardest thing in his life. He was never going down that road again. And he wasn't going to make promises he knew he couldn't hold to. It just wasn't his style, not now, not ever.

If he hadn't had his business to pour his energies into when Renata had died he may as well have buried himself with her. In some ways he probably had, but it was a choice he'd made, and one he stuck to.

He spun out of his chair and headed for the shower in the old bathroom of the converted Art Deco building, thankful—not for the first time—that he'd kept a fully functional bathroom in the office building. It gave him no end of pride to base the administrative side of his work here—his first completed project—the one his father had said would never succeed.

The house had been in a sorry state of repair, stuck in the middle of what had once been a residential area and which had slowly been absorbed by the nearby light-industrial zone. It had been just the sort of project he'd needed to get his hands on, literally, and had given him the opportunity to showcase his talents to restore and convert historical buildings for practical as well as aesthetic means. Cavaliere Developments had come a long way from the fledgling business he'd created eight years ago—and had a long way further to go if he had any say in the matter.

As he peeled off his work clothes, bunching them into a large crumpled ball in his fists, he wondered for the hundredth time if maybe he hadn't bitten off more than he could chew with the Sellers project. Buying the building outright wasn't the problem, he could do that without a blip on his financial radar. But converting it to luxury apartments, reminiscent of the era the building was constructed, took serious bucks. Bucks his board of directors, now headed by his father, would never authorise.

He'd worked out a way he could do it, though, a way to skip past any potential stonewalling by the board, and had liquidated everything he owned—his house, his stock in his father's company—everything, except his car and this building. He'd even temporarily moved in with his other brother, Mason, to minimise his expenses. But without the buffer of more funds his dream would be out of the running before he could even begin.

Declan rued, not for the first time, how easily he'd let his father take control of the board of directors when Renata died. How, in his grief, he'd let Tony Knight capitalise on his situation and take the seat of power for the one thing Declan had left that still meant anything. The old man had called most of the shots ever since. The board would never sanction taking on a loan the size he needed to make this job work.

But he had to make it work. He just had to. Somehow he'd get his hands on the money to make this dream come alive. After that, he'd resume control of his own company. It was all that mattered anymore, that and ensuring that he never laid himself open to being so weak that he'd lose control ever again.

Gwen Jones snapped her cell phone shut in frustration and drummed her fingers on the steering wheel of her car. If she couldn't put a halt to her wedding proceedings she'd be out of more than the deposits, she'd be out of her home, too. It had been Steve's idea to mortgage her house, and she'd reluctantly agreed, on the condition they only draw down sufficient funds to cover the wedding and some additional renovation costs on the late-nineteenth-century villa. But now he'd drawn down the lot and skipped the country. She'd never be able to cover the repayments on her own and she'd be forced to sell the only true home she'd ever known.

How could he do this to her?

Gwen flipped the phone open again and stabbed at the numbers, silently willing her maid-of-honour and hostess for tonight's celebrations, Libby, to be off the line. But for the sixth time in a row she went straight to Libby's answer phone, and there was no point in leaving another, even more frantic, message. Worse, there was no one answering at Cavaliere Developments. Even the cell number given in the message at Cavaliere rang unanswered before switching to the out-of-office auto service.

She raked impatient fingers through her long blond hair and tried to ignore the burning sensation in her stomach. Somehow, she had to be two places at once—but which was the most important? Cancelling her pre-wedding party for the forty or so friends Steve had said they couldn't afford to invite to the wedding, and which was due to start within the hour, or telling Declan Knight that his finance manager, *her fiancé,* had just fled the country after clearing out Cavaliere Developments' bank account along with her own?

There was no contest. As much as she dreaded facing him, she had to tell Declan.

She shifted gear and crawled another half metre forward, cursing once more Auckland's southern motorway gridlock that held her helpless in its grip, and tried to console herself the Penrose exit was only a short distance away.

By the time she pulled her station wagon up at the

kerb outside Cavaliere Developments' offices the sharp
burning in her stomach had intensified. She slammed
her car door shut and, walking with short swift steps to
the front of the building, popped an antacid from the roll
in her bag.

Declan Knight hated her already, but when he heard
what Steve had done… They didn't still shoot the mes-
senger, did they? Her stomach gave a vicious twist,
wrenching a small gasp of pain from her throat. She had
to pull herself together.

The sparsely designed single-storey building, so
typical of houses built in New Zealand during the late
twenties, loomed in front of her. The old front lawn had
been converted into car parks, but some of the gardens
had been kept and edged the front of the building.
Standard roses and gardenias scented the summer
evening air.

She forced one foot in front of the other until she
reached the entrance and dragged a steadying breath
deep into her lungs before pushing open the front door
to the reception area.

"Hello?" She waited, one hand clutching the straps
of her bag while the other settled against her stomach
as if doing so could calm the galloping herd of Kaima-
nawa wild horses that pranced there.

Nothing.

He had to be here. His distinctive classic Jag was still
parked in the driveway that ran down the side of the
house. Steve had just about bent her ear off covetously
extolling the virtues of the black 1949 XK120. She
could recite every statistic about the vehicle, from its
butter-soft leather upholstery to the horsepower rating
under the hood. The car was the perfect accessory for

the man Declan Knight had become and the man Steve, she now knew, had envied with every bone in his body. With Declan's aura of success, devilish smile, long hair and cover-model body, he was a must on every society matron's guest list and came complete with a different woman for every day of the week.

Quite a different guy to the one Renata had so excitedly introduced her to just over eight years ago. Quite a different guy to the one who, blinded by grief, had reached for her in the awful dark days after Renata's death, and then, with the lingering scent of their passion still in the air, had accused her of seducing him. He had cut her as effectively from his life as a surgeon removes a cancerous growth.

Her mouth flooded with bitterness at the memory. She swallowed against the sour taste and resolutely pushed the past aside. Their actions had been a complete betrayal of Renata's memory. Thinking about it sure wouldn't help now. The only thing she could do was fulfil the promise she'd made as Renata sliced through the rope that threatened to pull them both to their deaths—to look out for Declan where she'd failed to do so for her dead friend.

Gwen looked around the empty reception area. For a Friday it was unnaturally quiet, but, of course, instead of hanging back for an end-of-week drink, everyone was on their way to her party. Everyone except the groom. She had to get through this as quickly as possible and then let Libby know the wedding was off. Oh, Lord, today was a total nightmare with no respite within her grasp.

She popped another antacid and her heart skittered in her chest. Maybe she'd even missed Declan altogether—he could've taken a ride with someone else. No, not with the front door still unlocked, she rationalised.

Focus, she admonished herself, *you can't afford the luxury of falling apart now.* Gwen gripped the handle of her bag and strode through the front reception and down the hallway that led to the private offices. She hesitated as she reached the office Steve had used. At the lightest touch the door swung open.

It looked so normal inside. No clue to show that the man who'd worked here until lunchtime today had been on the verge of fleeing the country, his job and his fiancée. She pulled the door shut behind her, wishing she could as effectively close the door on her troubles. She wouldn't find the help she needed here.

Somewhere at the back of the house she heard a faucet snap closed.

"Hello? Is anyone here?" she called out.

As she reached the end of the hallway an erratic squeaking penetrated the air, as if someone was wiping a cloudy mirror with his hand. She laid her ear against the nearest door. The noise peppered the silence again with its staccato screech, setting her teeth on edge. She hesitated, her hand resting against the painted surface of the door. Should she knock?

Suddenly the door swung inwards, pulling her off balance. Wham! She crashed face first against a bare wall of male torso. She dropped her handbag in shock and her hands flung upwards to rest against a bare chest. Her senses filled with the aroma of lightly spiced, warm, damp skin, dizzying her with its subtle assault. Of their own accord, her eyes fastened to the slow rise and fall of the broad, tanned expanse of skin in front of her. To the flat brown nipples that suddenly contracted beneath her gaze.

Declan Knight. She remembered the taste of him as if it were yesterday.

Her gaze dropped swiftly over muscled contours and her breath caught in her throat. Please don't let him be naked. A rapid sigh of relief gusted past her lips at the view of a fluffy white towel wrapped low around his hips. A tiny droplet of water followed the shadowed line of his hip and arrowed slowly downwards.

Her mouth dried.

With Herculean effort she willed her eyes to work their way up—past the well-developed pectoral muscles, up the column of a strong masculine neck, where strands of glistening black hair caressed powerful shoulders, and all the way to where they finally clashed with cold, obsidian-coloured eyes.

He still held her. The gentle clasp of his long fingers belied the burning imprint that scorched through the filmy sleeves of her blouse and contrasted against the chilled disdain in his gaze. Fingers that tightened almost painfully as he recognised just who he held.

He let go rapidly, leaving her to find her own balance. "What the hell are you doing here?"

He looked as though he wanted to get straight back into the shower stall after touching her. Heat burned a wild bloom of colour across her cheeks and anger rose swift and sharp from the pit of her belly. Her fingers curled into impotent fists at her side.

"I'm fine, thank you for asking." Gwen reached up one hand and rubbed absently at her arm, although the movement only served to highlight the absence of his touch rather than negate it. "I need to talk to you—it's important."

"Go and wait out the front. I'll be with you in a minute."

"Right. Of course. I'll do that then." Gwen retrieved her handbag from by her feet and stormed back to the reception area, her heart hammering in her chest. What was wrong with her? Where was her brain? She really had to pull it together.

Slowly she counted to ten, focusing on each inward and outward breath. It was a simple strategy, and effective. One she'd perfected when she'd first arrived in New Zealand, from Italy, at nine years old—abandoned to the care of a disapproving maiden aunt by her capricious mother, who preferred her jet-set lifestyle without a child to hinder her liaisons.

"Steve's not here."

Gwen flinched at the sound of his voice and turned to face her nemesis. He'd obviously roughly towel-dried his hair, and although he'd dressed quickly he hadn't taken the time to dry himself properly. The fine cotton of his dress shirt clung in patches like a second skin to his damp skin. She snapped her eyes away, drew her back up as straight as she could manage and lifted her chin to meet his penetrating regard head-on.

Despite working within the same industry, they'd managed to avoid making contact on more than a cursory social level. Even on those occasions, at company functions, they'd managed to avoid having to be polite to one another. A cursory nod of acknowledgement, a not-quite-there smile when in a group of colleagues. They'd kept their distance. Distance he was obviously equally determined to maintain.

"I know." Her voice sounded as though it came from a stranger. Stilted, forced. Now that the time had come, the words dried up uselessly in her throat.

"So why are you here? If this is supposed to be one of those face-your-past things before you get married—"

"No! Oh, God, no. Definitely not." How could he

even think she wanted to bring *that* up again? The humiliating rejection after they'd futilely sought comfort in one another. She never wanted to cross that road again. Ever.

She watched as he pulled a vibrantly coloured, rolled up silk tie from his trouser pocket and threaded it underneath his collar. Gwen cleared her throat of the obstruction that threatened to choke her as she remembered just how dexterous those long fingers could be. How she'd been at their absolute mercy.

"Steve's gone," she blurted in an attempt to clear her mind of the sensual fog that clouded her thoughts.

"Gone? What are you talking about? We're all supposed to be at your party in about—" he broke off to look at his watch.

"About thirty minutes."

"So, we'll see him there. What's the problem?" Halfway through settling the knot of his tie at the base of his throat, his hands stilled. Her eyes still locked on his hands, Gwen stared at the slightly roughened edges of his fingers, evidence that given the opportunity he was as hands-on as any of his workers, at the graze across the knuckle on his index finger. At anything but the question in his eyes.

"Steve's left the country." The words tasted like charcoal in her mouth.

"Left the country?"

"With all our money. Yours and mine."

"That's ridiculous."

Gwen held her ground. She only wished she was kidding. Sudden seriousness chased the derisive look from Declan's face as his eyes raked her face for any sign of a lie.

"You're not kidding, are you?"

She shook her head slowly. The sting of moisture pricked at the back of her eyes and she pressed her lips into a firm line, blinking back the urge to let loose her fears.

"When? How?"

"He left a message on my cell. I was working in the Clevedon Valley—there's no reception—he knew I wouldn't get the call until I came out of the black spot. By then it was too late to stop him."

"You're saying he rang to tell you this? Why would he do that?"

Steve's gloating satisfaction replayed in her mind. She'd never forget that tone in his voice, the absolute glee that he'd gotten away with it combined with the fact that he'd known all along there'd been something between her and Declan in the past. He'd found a way to hurt them both. The man he'd most wanted to be and the woman he'd thought Declan still wanted. But he'd been wrong. Totally wrong.

"Does it matter why he did it? The fact is he did. He's cleaned us both out!" Her hands twisted the strap of her handbag. Round and round until it resembled a piece of rag caught in a drill bit at high speed.

Declan swore under his breath and booted up the computer at the front desk. His fingers flew over the keyboard as he logged onto his bank's Internet service, then stilled as the reality sunk in.

"I'm gonna kill the bastard." His voice low, feral.

"Well, take a number and stand in line. You'd better call the police. If you'll excuse me, I have a party to stop and a wedding to cancel." She pivoted on her heels and walked back out the door, half expecting any minute for him to call out to her to stop. To say something, anything. But he didn't.

Minutes later, fighting to control the anger that surged and swirled inside him, Declan hung up the phone from the police. There was little that could be done right now. He'd visit the station first thing in the morning.

He drummed his fingers on the desk, selecting and discarding ideas as to what to do next. Steve Crenshaw had single-handedly dealt the blow that could devastate Cavaliere Developments and put his entire staff out of work. Informing his board of directors would be the logical thing to do; no doubt the police would want to speak to them, too, once he'd formalised his statement.

He slammed his hands flat on the desk. *Damn!* To be so close, to be on the verge of success and have it all snatched away. That Gwen Jones had been the bearer of these particular bad tidings should have struck him as cruelly ironic. She was synonymous with everything that had gone wrong in his life in the past eight years.

It disturbed him a great deal more than he wanted to admit, seeing her so up close and personal just now—and to his absolute disgust his reaction hadn't been entirely emotional. All along, while Steve had crowed about his forthcoming nuptials he'd pushed away the thought of the other man's hands against Gwen's alabaster skin. But Declan had no claim on her—nor did he want one.

Still, her vulnerability struck him square in the solar plexus. She was as much a victim in this as him. More, in fact. She'd been on the verge of marrying the creep in eight days time. What did that say about her taste in men?

A flicker of an idea hovered on the periphery of his mind, then flamed to full-blown life. He'd be nuts to even consider it—but maybe that's exactly why it would work.

Despite everything, he would help Gwen Jones.

And whether she realized it now, or not, she would help him, too.

Gwen parked her station wagon in the secured basement parking allocated to Libby's waterfront apartment, then rode the lift to her floor. Outside the apartment the pain in Gwen's stomach wound up another notch. Judging by the racket on the other side of the door Libby hadn't had time to cancel the party—if she'd even retrieved Gwen's message by now. Gwen swiftly depressed the doorbell and turned away, forcing herself to take in a deep, steadying breath. The outlook through the massive window at the end of the corridor, over Auckland's Waitemata Harbour, usually had a calming effect on her, but tonight the city view glittered like tears reflected on the inky harbour, doing nothing to soothe her splintered thoughts.

"Gwen! Where the hell have you been?" Libby's voice penetrated the worry that encapsulated her brain. "And where's Steve?" she whispered, grabbing Gwen by the arm and dragging her inside.

"Libby, didn't you get my message? I need to talk to you. In private."

"Private? Sorry, chickie, but there's no privacy here." She threw out a hand to encompass the seething throng of guests.

"No, Libby. I mean it. We have to talk." She grabbed hold of Libby's arm, but the other woman slipped from her grasp.

"There's the door again, I'll be back in a minute. Here," she grabbed a glass of champagne from a tray full of filled glasses on the sideboard and pushed it into

Gwen's hand. "Wrap yourself around this while I see who it is. Maybe it's Steve."

Gwen put out a hand to stop her friend, but it was useless. Libby was on a roll and nothing short of a three-foot-thick plate of steel would halt her in full stride.

People pressed around. Many, colleagues of Steve's—some, her own clients she'd grown to like and respect. All of whom were oblivious to her turmoil and none of whom she knew well enough to slit an emotional vein and pour her news to, except Libby. Gwen scanned the room, nervously waiting for her friend to return. The babble of conversations seethed around her until she thought she would scream.

"Hey, everybody, look who's arrived!" Libby shouted above the crowd.

Heads turned, Gwen's included, as Declan was ushered into the room. His eyes searched the sea of heads, and Gwen pressed herself against the wall, as if she could make herself invisible by blending into the paintwork. Too late. He found her. He dropped a kiss on Libby's cheek and, with one of his killer smiles firmly on his face, started to work his way through the room, heading straight in her direction. People parted before him, like the Red Sea.

"Everyone, can I have your attention, please?" Libby's voice again rang out. Voices slowly stopped midconversation and all heads turned. "One of our guests of honour is here at last. The other's obviously running late, but in the meantime I'd like you all to charge your glasses in a toast to my favourite buddy and our bride-to-be."

Gwen felt the room tilt slightly as a sudden flurry of activity saw glasses rapidly being refilled in preparation for a toast. "No-o-o." The strangled protest was lost in the babble of noise around her.

Declan saw tension paint stark lines of fear on Gwen's face. His stomach tightened in a knot. He wasn't too late. Clearly Libby didn't know about Steve's desertion—yet.

A raised hand from Libby, obviously relishing playing hostess, drew the assembly to quiet again. "Now I know some of you haven't seen Gwen in a while, and I'm sure she joins me in thanking you for celebrating with us." She turned and bestowed a beaming, loving smile at her pale-faced friend. "Please, everyone, raise your glasses to Gwen. May you have many, many happy years."

"To Gwen!" Voices echoed all around her and multiple clinks of crystal repeated throughout the room. Declan watched as the remaining colour leached from Gwen's face, leaving it ghostly pale. She swayed slightly on legs that appeared to have become too weak to bear her slender frame.

An instinctive surge of protection billowed through him. He pressed forward, determined to reach her side before she collapsed. As his arm slipped around her waist a shout penetrated the air.

"So, where's your lucky man, Gwen?"

The tightly wound tension in her body transferred itself to him as all eyes swivelled to Gwen, who right now looked nothing like a radiant bride-to-be should. Sheer terror flew across her face, her colourless lips incapable of moving. The growing silence around them hung in the air like a fully charged rocket about to be launched.

As if suddenly aware of his presence she turned slightly towards Declan. Her eyes locked onto his, their shimmering grey depths reflecting a fierce combination of fear, distress and barely veiled entreaty.

Electricity curled through him, until he felt as though he crackled with unearthed energy. This was his opportunity. Decisively, he linked his free hand through the cold trembling fingers of hers. He drew them to his lips and brushed a kiss across the whitened knuckles.

His eyes still locked with hers, he pitched his voice to ring through the room.

"I'm right here."

Two

With only three short syllables Gwen was trapped in a nightmare that had grown to gargantuan proportions.

In shocking, sudden silence lipsticked mouths dropped open, eyebrows shot into hairlines and glasses of champagne raised in a toast remained clutched in hands still poised in the air. In the surreal atmosphere, all eyes turned to the tall, commanding presence of the man whose impossible response still reverberated through the room.

A bone-deep chill invaded Gwen's body and held her as still as a marble statue. This couldn't be happening. Not to her. She could get out of this. Surely all she had to do was laugh it off as a clever joke. Except she'd never felt less like laughing in her whole life.

The sureness of Declan's strong arm hooked around her waist sent warmth spreading through her body.

The sound of a single set of hands applauding drew Gwen's eyes to her friend Libby. *Nice surprise,* her friend mouthed silently, a grin spread across her face as wide as the Auckland Harbour Bridge. One by one, each of the guests joined in until cries of congratulations filled the room. People thronged around them, eager to pass on good wishes to the 'happy' couple. All the while Gwen kept a smile pasted to her face, leaving Declan to bear the brunt of the questions.

At some time, in the crush of perfumed bodies, he let go of her hand. Despite herself, she couldn't help but feel lost. Seeking out her friend, she found Libby leaning against the back wall of the room, a self-satisfied smile painted on her face.

"Well, you're a dark horse. Fancy not telling me!"

"I tried to talk to you when I got here. But, Libby, it's not what you think—"

"Whatever, Gwen. I'm thrilled to bits for you, but what about Steve? How did he take the news?"

"He... I..."

"He's taken an extended leave of absence," Declan interrupted, arriving like a dark shadow on Gwen's horizon. "We're sorry to have broken the news to you like this, Libby. We'd hoped to tell you sooner, hadn't we, hon?"

His eyes shot Gwen a dark challenge, underlying the steel in his voice, which warned her to agree, before he tucked her back against his side. Awareness of him, of every breath he took, seared through her thin clothing.

"Sometimes you absolutely know when it's right," he continued smoothly. "Besides, we've known each other for years and now we have the rest of our lives to find everything out about one another. Don't we?" He prompted her with a squeeze.

Gwen's mouth dried. He wasn't serious. He couldn't be. He could barely stand to be in the same room as her, yet now he'd become her latest fashion accessory. His strong fingers increased their pressure under her rib cage, reminding her she had to make a response. She swallowed, trying to moisten her throat and allow the words that were trapped inside to come out.

"Y-yes." Good Lord! Was that her voice?

A tiny frown creased between Libby's eyebrows. "Gwen? Are you certain you're doing the right thing?"

Gwen drew in a deep breath. "Yes."

Thank goodness. Her voice was stronger now. More definite, although she'd never felt more adrift in her entire life.

Declan dipped his head to her temple. "Good move." His warm lips moved intimately against her skin. To anyone in the room it looked like a caress.

"If you're certain..." Libby's voice trailed away, doubt still clear in her tone.

"We've never been more certain of anything in our lives." Declan's voice resonated confidence. "Do you mind if we have a moment together, in private? You will excuse us, won't you?"

"Certainly. Why don't you use my bedroom?" Libby offered generously—too generously in Gwen's opinion.

"No!" Gwen's voice shot like a bullet. "I mean, the balcony will do fine. No one will bother us out there."

The last thing she needed was to be in a bedroom with Declan Knight. She pulled free of his clasp, once again struck by an inane sense of loss, and stumbled slightly as the heel of her strappy sandal hooked on the thickly carpeted floor. A strong grip at her elbow steadied her. Did he have to be so constantly close he could touch her?

"Okay?" He reached past her to open the glass slider that led onto the semicircular balcony.

"I'm fine. At least, I will be once we sort this mess out."

She turned, freeing herself from his hold and tried to ignore the glow of challenge that lit his eyes at her action. A glow that was doing funny things to her sensitive stomach. More indigestion, she decided. Except this felt different. It was a fire in her belly all right, but this burn was molten, enticing and as forbidden as it had been eight years ago.

Declan slid the door closed behind them, the double-glazed floor-to-ceiling windows cutting out almost all sound from inside. Marooned on a dark island, the shimmer of lights reflected across the harbour.

"What do you want to sort out first?" He crossed his arms over the broad expanse of his chest and leaned back against the waist-high concrete wall that scalloped the balcony. Backlit by the streetlights behind him, he towered there, large and powerful. His dark head haloed like some fallen angel.

"Our *engagement* for one thing. What the heck are you playing at? I don't want to marry you and I know for certain you don't want to marry me, either."

"You're right. But the way I see it, it's the perfect solution to our problems."

"Don't be ridiculous. How on earth could our marriage be a solution to anything? We've barely even spoken since Renata died." Spoken? No. But they had done so much more.

"This has nothing to do with Renata." He bit the

words out. She could see the tension drawn on his face, the hardening of his jaw. "Smile."

"What?" Had he lost his mind?

"Smile. Everyone inside can see us and we've just announced our engagement. They expect you to look happy, not as if you'd like to tip me over this balcony."

"Don't tempt me," she answered, her voice low and angry. The thought had sudden appeal, but instead of seeing Declan tumbling from the balcony all she had was a vivid memory of Renata's body tumbling past her on the rock face that had almost sent them both to their doom. No, she couldn't joke about that, not even for a minute. Gwen forced her lips into an approximation of a smile.

"That's better." Declan's voice rumbled through the dark night air. "Now come over here and put your arms around me."

"No way." A chill shivered over her arms, raising goose bumps on her flesh, belying the warmth of the balmy humid evening.

"Then I'll come over to you."

Before she could protest Declan covered the short distance between them, draped her limp arms around his waist and linked his own around hers.

"There now, that didn't hurt a bit."

Hurt? Maybe not in the physical sense, but there was an ache deep down inside her that had been her constant companion for longer than she wanted to acknowledge. A pain that couldn't be assuaged and had taken eight years to learn to ignore. Damn him for opening that wound again.

"So, are you happy now?" Her words dropped bitterly from her lips.

"Hardly. This is all for show. If we're going to make this work we have to look the part."

"Make it work? I haven't even agreed to this charade. In case you hadn't already noticed I'm supposed to be engaged to Steve," she snapped. His arms were warm bands around her, his fingers stroking in lazy circles against the small of her back. Gwen forced herself to listen to him and to ignore the spirals of pleasure that radiated traitorously from his touch.

"I believe that could be disputed, considering he's abandoned you to face the wedding without him. Besides, you're not exactly heartbroken he's gone. Angry at him, for sure. He's cleaned you out. But heart-broken? I doubt it."

Gwen flinched as the truth in his words cut her to her core. Yes, Steve had abandoned her, but worse, Declan was right. With Steve she'd thought she could be safe. After all, wasn't that what had attracted her to him in the first place? No crazy emotions living on the surface of their life. No wild declarations of burning passion. He'd been a biddable man. Someone she could rely on, or so she'd thought. A man who would be a reliable father and a supportive partner. *A man who sounds about as exciting as a well-made foundation garment,* a little voice taunted from the back of her mind.

Gwen gathered what was left of her dignity. "Look, I'll tell Libby the truth when everyone is gone. She'll help me call around, cancel the wedding. It was only going to be small. It won't take long."

A vise clamped around her chest. What the heck was she going to do then? Thanks to Steve, she didn't even have enough left in her account to buy groceries—let alone meet the demands of the loan now secured against

the house that had been part of her family for genera-
tions. A swell of nausea rocked her. She was going to
lose her home—her one bastion of security since the day
her mother had shucked her off like last year's fashion.

Declan interrupted her misery. "So don't cancel."

Gwen reached deep to draw the courage she needed
to answer him. "Give me one good reason why I should
want to pretend to be engaged to you."

"There's no *pretend* about it. We will get married.
Under New Zealand law we have just enough time to
make your original wedding date, too."

"Did you slip and bang your head or something?"
Gwen leaned back slightly, deliberately ignoring the
contact of her hips against his lower body, and looked
hard in his eyes. "There's no way I'm marrying you."

"Yes, you are. Look, it's certainly not my idea of the
ideal solution, either, but right now it's the only way
you're going to get your money back. As your husband,
I can make sure of that."

Gwen was lost for words. Even though the reality of
Steve's defection had only just begun to sink in, some
glimmer of hope still clung to the thought that she'd get
the money back from him, somehow.

"The way I see it," Declan continued, "we both stand
to benefit from a wedding."

"No—"

"Hear me out. Once Crenshaw's found, I *will* find a
way to get the money back, you can count on it. But in
the meantime his actions have put me in a very difficult
position. You've heard about the Sellers tender?"

Gwen nodded. She'd more than heard about it. She'd
been eagerly awaiting the outcome of the sale tender for
the Art Deco hotel in the hope it would be redeveloped

in keeping with its distinctive history. Then she could put in a proposal of her own to subcontract to the successful company. With her expertise in the restoration of old furnishings, and her skill in sourcing the materials required to redecorate to suit the period of the properties she'd worked on, she was in high demand. But a contract like the Sellers Hotel—that would launch her into an entirely new sphere altogether.

"I've put a bid together to purchase the property, but no thanks to Steve's creative accounting I'll have to withdraw from the tender unless I have the funds to continue the development—unless I can get my hands on a hefty sum of money. Now, I have that money at my disposal, but the only way I can access it is to marry. And that's where you come in." He dipped his head closer to hers, his dark eyes boring into her own. For all intents and purposes, to the guests whose buzz of conversation filtered in muffled snatches through the glass door to the balcony, they looked like a couple in love. The length of his legs seared through the fabric of her skirt. The outline of his muscled thighs and the weight of his hips pressed against her. Logic demanded she pull back, loose herself from his grasp and denounce his crazy idea for the fraud it was. To get the wild beat of her heart back under control.

"You have to marry? That's archaic," Gwen protested.

"It's the way it is. My mother was a traditionalist and wanted to see all her boys settled before accessing our trust funds."

A trust fund he'd already have had access to if she hadn't let Renata talk her into attempting that cliff face when it was way beyond Gwen's experience. But she couldn't let her guilt at Renata's death drive her into making yet another mistake. "And how would this advantage me? All I can see is a win-win for you here. Getting married isn't just something you do to access a trust fund, for goodness sakes! No, it's too important. I can't—I won't do it."

"I'll repay the money Steve stole from you."

Gwen pulled out of his arms and walked across the balcony until she could go no farther from him. Declan felt the loss of her form against his body as if she'd been carved from him. As much as he denied it, they fit well together. Too well. In the evening darkness he studied her face carefully, watching as emotions chased across its surface until an implacable calm replaced the confusion. "C'mon, Gwen. What do you say?"

"I don't want to do this."

"It's gone beyond what we *want* to do, Crenshaw's seen to that. We need to make a decision, Gwen. Tonight."

"Why do we have to do all this? Why can't you just take out a business loan?" Light from a streetlamp caressed her white-blond hair and silhouetted her slender shape against the darkness like a sculptor's loving touch.

"Because I wouldn't get the loan."

"Don't be ridiculous. Cavaliere Developments is one of the most successful and fastest-growing companies in the industry. Even I know that."

Declan clenched his fists at his sides, then released his fingers, one by one. He had to convince Gwen, and the only way out was the truth, no matter how much it hurt. "When Renata died I had to keep busy, keep moving, keep working. I didn't have the necessary capital then to expand at the rate I wanted to for the company to gain a foothold in the marketplace, nor did I want to spend the time I needed on the business end of things. All I wanted was to be so dog tired by the end of each day that I couldn't even think any more." He rubbed a hand across his eyes. The pain of that time still as raw in his memory as the day he'd laid Renata's broken body to rest. He drew in a ragged breath and pressed on. "The old man stepped in, offered to act as guarantor for me and help run things from the administration side, *if* I gave him a voting position on the board. It was only supposed to be for a limited time."

"I don't understand. Why would that stop your company from getting the contract?" Gwen's question hung in the air, her confusion evident in her tone.

"Because he's already made it clear he'll veto any application for funds for a project this size. He likes to control people. He likes to think he can control me."

"And if you have the trust fund?" she prompted.

"I can bankroll the whole project myself." *Please don't let her say no.*

"I see. I imagine there are a lot of jobs riding on this, too."

"Yes, there are."

Her shoulders sagged as if all the air had been drawn out of her.

"All right." Her reply was a mere ripple of sound in the night air.

"You'll do it?" Hope leaped in his chest.

"Yes, but only on certain conditions."

"What sort of conditions?"

She paced the width of the balcony before coming to a halt in front of him again. "You contract me to work on the Sellers building for the duration of the refit."

He could live with that. In fact he was more than

happy with the agreement. She'd made her mark in domestic restorations but with her skill she could only benefit his operation. Despite how he felt about Gwen, he was enough of a businessman to recognise an advantage when he saw it.

"Done. We'll sort out the nuts and bolts of your contract with Connor tomorrow and get this tied up legally. Don't worry about him knowing, he can be trusted to keep our arrangement confidential. Anything else?"

"No sex."

Declan arched one eyebrow. "Do you mean with anybody else, or just with each other?"

"With anybody. I mean it," she reiterated fiercely, wrapping her arms about her body like armour. "Absolutely no sex. I won't be made a fool of. If this marriage is to look real, then you can't see anyone else."

Yeah, well, he could live with that, too. In fact, he was more than happy to live with that. The one time…no, it didn't bear thinking about. It was enough that she had agreed to go along with this crazy scheme. "Fine by me. But we have to look like a married couple when we're around other people, be comfortable together, you know—physically. Especially around the rest of my family. They might accept this sudden engagement, but they'll suspect a sham if we don't behave like a newly wed couple, and if my dad suspects a sham, I can kiss that trust fund goodbye."

"Won't they ask questions anyway?"

"Probably. But that's my problem. I'll handle it." He sighed. "Anything else?"

"About the financial terms of the contract…"

Declan had had enough. "It'll be worth your while— I promise."

"It had better be." Her eyes were opaque pools of emptiness. What was going on in that head of hers?

"It's a deal, then?" He had to be certain she wasn't going to back out of this.

"One more thing."

He bit back an expletive. She had him between a rock and a hard place, and he hated it. Hated being beholden to her. "What is it?" Amazingly the words sounded civil.

"The length of our marriage—three months, tops."

"Three months! That's ridiculous. Twelve or my father will definitely smell a rat."

"That's far too long. Six, then."

"Six months?" Declan considered it for a moment—that would work, just. He nodded sharply.

Gwen extended her hand to him and he took it, noting this was the first time she'd voluntarily reached out and touched him, tonight anyway. Laughter from inside penetrated the glass, reminding him they were in full view of the party going on inside. He turned her hand slightly, noting the tracery of blue veins beneath the silver-pale skin at her wrist. He bent forward and lifted her wrist to his lips, pressing them against satin skin where her pulse beat frantically, like a captured butterfly. She clearly wasn't as unmoved as she tried to project.

"Just keeping up appearances," he smiled grimly when she yanked her hand away as though his touch had burned her. "Oh, and Gwen?"

"What?"

"Thank you. You won't regret it."

"Regret it?" Gwen gave a sharp laugh as she turned to go inside. "I already do."

Three

"Well, this certainly is an interesting turn of events." Libby spoke from behind, her voice making Gwen jump. She needed to get a grip on these jitters. She was as skittish as a first time buyer at an auction.

"Don't tease, Libby, it isn't kind."

"So, come on, how long has this been going on?" her friend drawled with a wink.

"Not long. It kind of took us both by surprise." She clenched her hands at her sides, hoping Libby wouldn't press her further. From the corner of her eye she saw Declan come back into the room—his presence effortlessly dominating the gathering.

Despite the way he'd treated her since Renata's death, her gaze was continually drawn to him like metal filings to a magnet. The sensation of his lips still throbbed against her wrist. Unfortunately it was proving a great deal more difficult than she wanted to return her heartbeat to a regular rhythm. She couldn't believe she'd agreed to go ahead with this. It didn't take a rocket scientist to figure out the whole situation wouldn't work. There was still too much that lay between them. Forget the frying pan. She was jumping straight into the fire.

Libby pursed her lips and let out a low whistle, "He's welcome to take me by surprise any day of the week. No objections here, chickie!"

Gwen forced a laugh through her lips, although her face felt as if it would crack if she tried any harder. All at once the tension of the day became unbearable and exhaustion struck her in waves.

"You know, I would never have picked you for his type," Libby continued.

Gwen felt an unexpected pang. Didn't her friend think she was up to the job? "Really?" Her voice was glacial.

Remorse chased across Libby's face as she realised how her words had sounded. "Oh, heck, Gwen. I'm sorry. I didn't mean it the way that came out. But you know he certainly hasn't been short of female company in the past few years."

"It's okay."

But deep inside, Libby's words struck home. Gwen had been the antithesis of Renata—cool and controlled when her friend had been full of fire and unpredictable. Since that dreadful night, after Renata's funeral, he'd made it clear he wanted her the hell out of his life. As time had gone by Declan had been surrounded by female admirers of all ages and marital persuasions. So why ask her when he must have any number of eager candidates to help him access his trust fund? Unless it was because he knew he'd never make the mistake of falling in love with her. Somehow, the realization only made her feel worse.

"Are you okay, Gwen? You look all done in."

"It's been a heck of a day. I'll be fine after a good night's sleep." Gwen crossed her fingers in the wild hope that it might be so simple. "I think I'd better head off, thanks for tonight."

"I'll see you home." The two women wheeled at the sound of Declan's voice. Before she could object, they'd said their goodnights and the warm, firm pressure of his hand at the small of her back was herding her out the door and down the carpeted corridor to the elevator bank.

As soon as the elevator arrived Gwen stepped in, distancing herself from the steady warmth emanating from Declan's body. In the aftermath of tonight it would have been so easy to simply lean back against his strength, but Gwen had learned her lesson, and learned it the hard way. She couldn't rely on any man, especially Declan Knight.

"I have my car here, you know," she said as she moved away from the console of push buttons, leaving him to depress the ground floor button. "I can see myself home."

"We'll collect it tomorrow. Besides, you're my fiancée. People would wonder why we didn't go home together, especially tonight." His tone was mildly teasing, but did nothing to relax her.

The ride to the ground floor was mercifully brief. Gwen stepped into the apartment building foyer anxious to clear her lungs of the subtle, yet enticing, fragrance he wore. A scent that made her want to bury her face at the base of his throat and inhale, deeply. To stroke the hollow at the base of his neck with the tip of her tongue and see if he tasted as good as he smelled—as good as she remembered. *Hold it right there!* she admonished swiftly. Don't let him invade your mind like that.

"So, where are you parked?" Her voice echoed, a brittle sound in the empty lobby.

"In the basement."

"Then why have we stopped at the ground floor?" Gwen went to get back in the lift.

Declan hooked one arm across her shoulders and steered her to the front door. "I thought we'd both benefit from a walk along the beach."

"It's late," she protested.

"Yeah, I know. And you need your beauty sleep. But you need to unwind more. C'mon, this'll only take a few minutes. Think of it as training for when we meet up with the rest of my family."

Smarting slightly from the beauty sleep remark, Gwen let him guide her across the road and through the grassy reserve on the other side. Once they reached the sandy width of beach she bent to slip off her shoes and suddenly wished she hadn't. Declan loomed over her, no mean feat when she topped five ten herself.

She felt small. Feminine. Vulnerable.

Despite the activity on the sidewalk, they were alone on the beach—entirely too intimate for comfort. Gwen jogged lightly to the water's edge, letting the iridescent foam lick over her toes and wash up to her ankles, taking refuge in the sudden chill on her heated skin. The late summer night air was gentle, laden with the combination of scents from the ocean in front of her and the restaurants that lined the road parallel to the beach. A warm breeze caressed her hair and lifted the long strands to dance flirtatiously across her cheeks and against her lips.

"What makes you think we can make this work?" she

asked, her voice carrying on the night breeze. She jumped as he replied from right behind her.

"We will. We have to."

The grim determination in his voice was daunting. He was right. Somehow, despite the past, they had to make this work. But at what price? A small rogue wave threatened to soak them both. He effortlessly swung her away, out of its path. There was that feeling again. Feminine. *Vulnerable.*

The breath whooshed from her lungs in a soft 'poof' as her breasts pressed softly against his chest and, irrationally, she wished she could be closer. Her pulse jumped like water on a hot skillet as the flats of his palms stoked across and down her long spine and over her hips. Flames of heat licked about her body where he'd touched, defying every instinctive warning in her mind. Without realising it her body melted against the hardness of his, moulding to every plane as if it belonged there even though nothing could be further from the truth.

Declan's hands whipped to her upper arms and he set her away from him, an indistinct oath barely emerging from his mouth.

"You okay?" His voice was a rumble from deep in his throat.

"I'm fine, thank you." She was a little breathless and a warm tide of blood had rushed to her cheeks at the sensation of his unyielding body against her softer curves. Her body had moulded to his as if they'd never been apart, as if they'd never betrayed Renata's memory— as if they, and not he and Renata, had belonged together. She turned away and walked carefully through the soft sand. Anything to create some distance from him and the decimating memories being with him evoked.

Declan slid out of his jacket, slung it over one shoulder and walked a few silent paces beside her. "We're marrying for the right reasons." His voice rumbled across the night air.

"Right reasons?" Gwen was startled. To her the right reasons were love, honour and respect. But then had she had all three in the forefront of her mind when she'd agreed to marry Steve? No. Safety, security and sameness. They'd been in the forefront of her mind, and look where that had got her. An ironic burst of laughter broke from her throat. "Care to name them?"

"Respect is one."

Her eyebrows lifted as he verbalised the one word she felt sure could never describe their relationship. "Respect? After...? No, sorry, you'll have to try harder than that. How can you say we have respect for one another?" The word couldn't be further from the truth—loathing on his part maybe, but respect? No way.

"I respect your professional integrity. That's what's important here. As for the rest, we know exactly where we stand. Both of us know it isn't a grand passion and we know it isn't forever. No broken promises, no broken hearts."

Gwen caught her lip between her teeth and stared out at the lights from the naval base blinking across the harbour. The burn of bitter rejection rose from her stomach. Could she do this? Oh, God, she hoped so. She couldn't afford not to. A sudden sheen of frustrated tears filmed Gwen's eyes. She blinked them away, furious at herself for almost exposing such weakness. She took a deep, steadying breath, then another. Finally satisfied she had her emotions under control she faced Declan. "Yes, of course. You're right. I'd like to go home now."

In silence they walked back across the road and to the ramp leading to the car park. As they approached the parking area Gwen halted in her steps.

"I'll take my own car home. Everyone saw us leave the party together so you don't have to worry about anyone suspecting that we didn't go home together, too." A strong hand on her arm stopped her in her tracks.

"I said I'll take you home and I will."

"But it isn't necessary. My car's here and I'll have to come back tomorrow to get it, anyway."

Declan slid his arm around her waist and turned her towards where his car waited. "Don't argue with me, Gwen. I always do what I say I'll do. We'll sort out your car tomorrow after we've seen Connor to iron out our contract."

While his vintage sports car ate up the distance to her home Gwen's mind raced as she mulled over the turn her life had suddenly taken. Her lips twisted ruefully— not even her mother could claim to have been engaged to two men in the same day. Okay, she decided, marrying Declan would suit her purposes—for now— and, quite clearly, would suit his also. Yes, it was cold-blooded to go into marriage like this, as if they'd brokered a deal, but once he'd uplifted his trust fund and she'd sorted out this financial mess Steve had left her in they could drift apart, and when they divorced no one would be hurt. Would they?

Sandpaper bit into her fingers as Gwen applied more pressure than was strictly necessary. One way or another she was going to make a difference to the carved mantelpiece she'd pried from her sitting room fireplace early this morning. Maybe, if she rubbed hard enough, she could erase not only the layers of paint that masked the natural native timber she hoped dwelled beneath, but also the fact her hard-won and carefully structured life had spiralled out of control.

Her stomach did an uncomfortable flip, sending a distinct reminder that skipping breakfast hadn't been such a wonderful thing to do.

Last night hung in her memory. She'd gone over it and over it in her mind, trying to see how she could have handled things differently. How she could have said "no." But no matter how many different scenarios she'd played, the outcome had remained the same.

During the ride to her Epsom home last night Declan had been quiet, only acknowledging her directions to find her house with the minimum of conversation. He'd seen her to the door but hadn't lingered. Gwen had half expected him to try and kiss her goodnight—only in the interests of maintaining the closeness they were going to have to make look natural, of course—and had suffered an odd pang of disappointment when he hadn't. A pang she certainly didn't want to examine too closely.

With a rueful sigh Gwen set the sandpaper aside— she was doing more damage than good with it, anyway. The years of paint layered on the mantel definitely required chemical intervention. She pushed a loose strand of hair from her face. If only heavy-duty paint stripper would solve all her problems.

Gwen jumped as a shadow fell over her shoulder.

"I knocked, but you obviously didn't hear me."

Declan! Gwen stood abruptly, too abruptly as the blood drained from her head and grey spots danced before her eyes. She blinked to clear them and took in a deep breath. Bad move, she scolded, as the enticing fragrance of man and subtle spice enveloped her senses. The scent of him had lingered with her long after he'd seen her to her front door last night. It had plagued her as she'd tossed about in her sheets, futilely seeking the refuge of slumber.

"You're a bit pale today," he commented, assessing her through narrowed eyes. "Not enough sleep?"

There was nothing wrong with his complexion nor, she noted in annoyance, anything else about him. He looked enticingly debonair in a black, short-sleeved cotton shirt and charcoal-grey trousers. He'd tied his long hair back, exposing the broad plane of his forehead and the cheekbones that should have looked ridiculous on a man, yet on him just served to make him look even more compelling.

She tried to ignore the way the fabric of his shirt draped across his shoulders and over his chest. The memory of how what lay beneath that finely woven fabric felt against her was still all too vivid. A millennia could pass and she'd still know the feel of him as intimately as she knew her own body.

"I suppose you slept like a baby?" Gwen snapped in retaliation.

"I did." His response left no doubt all was well with *his* world. "You've been busy this morning, I see." He raised his thumb to Gwen's cheek. "You should be wearing a mask, you know. That could be lead-based."

Fire branded her skin at his gentle touch, and she jerked her head back. "Most of my gear is in the back of my station wagon. I take it you're here to help me collect it?" She swiped her hands on the seat of her jeans before dusting her face, removing all remnants of the paint dust and the lingering trace of his touch.

"Later. We're going ring-shopping first."

"Ring-shopping?" Gwen took a step back. "Whatever for?"

"Our engagement, perhaps?" Declan raised one eyebrow.

"I don't need a ring." She had agreed with Steve a ring was an unnecessary purchase even though in her heart of hearts she would have enjoyed the possessive declaration of promise wearing his ring would have given her.

"Need doesn't come into it. We have to make this look believable and we don't have a lot of time. I'm buying you a ring. Why don't you go and get changed? Unless, of course, you'd prefer to go like that?" He gestured at her paint-stained shirt and faded jeans.

An imp of perversity almost induced her to insist on going in her work clothes. If she truly thought it would bother him, she would have done it. However, Declan didn't look at all perturbed by the idea. His attention had been grabbed by her current project.

"You're doing a good job on this mantelpiece. Are you going to brush paint stripper into these carvings?"

"Eventually. The stripper's in the back of my car." Gwen's lips thinned. If he hadn't insisted on bringing her home last night she could've made greater inroads on the mantel than she'd managed thus far.

"We can swing by Libby's and pick it up after we've been shopping. I'll follow you back and give you a hand if you like." He glanced at his watch. "We'd better hit the road. The jeweller doesn't usually open on a Saturday and he's making an exception for us today."

Give her a hand? Gwen reassessed his muscled shoulders. She may as well resign herself to the fact he was going to be around and put him to good use. There was nothing distinctly romantic about renovation. So far, and with little help from Steve, who'd preferred to keep his apartment when they'd become engaged, it had been sheer hard graft. Besides, she reasoned, it would serve to desensitise her to the crazy lurch she felt deep inside every time Declan came within three feet of her.

Gwen's stomach growled, loud enough to tease another half smile from Declan's lips.

"Maybe I should feed you first?"

"I'm fine," she retorted. "I'll be ready in five minutes."

After choosing and discarding at least six different outfits, she was ready in fourteen.

"Let's get this over with." She slung her bag over her shoulder and reached up to twist her hair into a silver clip. Dressed in shades of lavender and deep plum Gwen knew, aside from the shadows under her eyes even concealer couldn't hide, she looked good. And for reasons she didn't want to examine too deeply, it was important that she did.

"You make it sound like pulling teeth would be more fun." Declan pulled his keys from his pocket but didn't make any move to leave.

"You said it, not me."

"Why are you so angry?" He barred the doorway with one arm, effectively preventing her from avoiding the question. "It's only a ring."

"Shall we go?" Gwen gave him a pointed stare before ducking under his arm and taking swift steps down the hall to the front door.

"Okay, so you don't want to talk about it." Declan followed with a measured tread. "You know, it would make things easier if you'd relax a little."

"I'm perfectly fine." She held the door open as he passed through and took her time securing the deadlock.

Declan laughed. "If you say so."

At the kerbside his car gleamed—dark, long and low. He had the top down today, making the most of the calm fine weather. He held her door open until she was settled, lifted the trailing hem of her skirt, tucking it gently by her legs. In the confines of the passenger seat it was impossible to pull away from him. She tried to ignore the way her heartbeat had accelerated at the brush of his fingers against her calf.

The car was a beauty. Last night she'd been too lost in her own thoughts to pay much attention to the vehicle or observe its power—cloaked in sensuous sleek lines much like its owner's—or to recognize how perfectly it matched him.

Classical beauty. Power. Danger.

Steve had driven a company sedan. Practical, he'd said when he'd driven it home. But even then she'd seen how he'd eyed Declan's car—his resentment carefully veiled beneath the surface, she realised now.

Gwen stroked the soft leather seat. "She's beautiful."

"Yeah." Declan settled behind the wheel, his eyes trapping her with dark intensity as he faced her. "She is."

Gwen didn't quite know where to look, or what to say. Her fingers curled into her palms, her short sensible nails pressing into her skin with increasing pressure until he turned and slipped the key into the ignition and brought the engine to roaring life.

Her eyes widened a short while later when she recognized the scripted gold lettering on the rich burgundy-coloured awning outside the jewellers' store.

"I don't think this is a good idea," she protested as Declan rolled the Jag to a halt.

"Why not?"

"This place…" she hesitated, lost for words.

"Yeah?" he prompted. "What about it?"

"It's too expensive—can't we try somewhere else?" She suggested a popular chain of jewellers, noted for their mass-produced designs.

"If we're going to do this, and convince everyone it's real, we have to do it right. C'mon, it'll be okay. I promise you won't see a price tag anywhere."

"That's the trouble," she muttered under her breath as he came around the car and opened her door.

Inside, the store was elegant and serene. Faint strains of Vivaldi penetrated the air. Carefully designed lighting accented the select number of stunning pieces on display.

"Ah, Declan! Congratulations my friend and, of course, you also, mademoiselle." A tall, thin man with slightly stooped shoulders strode through the show-room. "I was beginning to despair my old friend would ever take advantage of my expertise."

"Give it a rest, Frank." Declan accepted the other man's proffered hand and gave it a quick, solid shake. "Let me introduce you both. Gwen, this is my old school buddy, Frank Dubois. Frank, meet my future wife, Gwen Jones."

"*Enchanté*, Miss Jones." The jeweller smiled, warmth lighting his eyes.

"Please, call me Gwen."

"And you must call me François. Don't listen to this cretin, he refused always to learn French correctly."

Gwen struggled to hide a laugh. She'd never heard *anyone* refer to Declan Knight as a cretin.

"Hey, enough of the disrespect, Frank. I'm a customer today," Declan reminded him.

"Yes, and I'm certain I have just the thing you might

be looking for. A platinum setting I think, with Gwen's colouring. Yes, come with me."

François led them to a back room, where he removed a tray of rings from a locked drawer.

Gwen was temporarily dazzled by the display of coloured stones all in a variety of settings. François picked an oval-cut pink sapphire ringed in brilliant diamonds.

"No," Declan stated flatly. "That's not it. I want her to have diamonds only."

The jeweller nodded slightly and replaced the tray in its drawer before sliding another under Declan's watchful gaze.

"Yes. This is it." Declan sounded well satisfied.

From the bed of black velvet he picked out a large marquise-cut diamond ring, set with three tapered-baguette diamonds on each side. It was a stunning piece and she watched, mesmerised, as he slid the ring on her finger.

"Perfect fit," he pronounced. "What do you think?"

"It's…it's…" Gwen faltered.

"There's a matching wedding band." François extracted a channel-set baguette diamond wedding band from the tray.

Gwen was overwhelmed. The rings were stunning pieces of workmanship. But they simply weren't her. Words failed her but actions didn't. She pulled her hand from Declan's and tried to remove the ring. It fit so snugly she had difficulty manoeuvring it back over her knuckle.

"I don't think so," she finally managed.

"No?" Declan asked. "You'd prefer something bigger?"

"Oh, no! Definitely not. The ring is lovely, in fact they all are, but I don't feel right about any of them."

"Okay." Declan took the ring from her and handed it

back to François. "Sorry, mate. Looks like we opened you up for nothing."

"Don't worry, *mon ami*. We're expecting a new shipment of diamonds early in the next week. Perhaps we can design something special for you both."

Gwen wandered back into the showroom, where brightly lit display cases showcased certain items.

"Oh," she sighed involuntarily as she caught sight of a ring so beautiful in its simplicity it called out to her.

"Have you seen something you like?" Declan joined her at the display case. "Frank, come over and open this up."

"Ah, one of our estate pieces bought in Europe last month," François explained as he disarmed the sensor in the case and removed the plain, emerald-cut diamond ring from its pedestal. "If you like antique pieces I have many more I can show you."

"No," Declan said, with a watchful eye on Gwen's face as she tried on the ring. "This is the one, isn't it?"

Only a ring, he'd said back at the house. That's all it was. Only a ring. So why did her heart absolutely sing with pleasure at the sight of it? Why did it feel so right on her finger?

"Gwen?" Declan prompted.

"Yes. I love it."

"It's yours, then, and a wide plain wedding band, too, I think Frank."

"And what about you, *mon ami?* Are we looking for a band for you also?"

Gwen held her breath. Would he, too, wear a ring? Steve had refused one, saying they didn't need the added expense. Suddenly the prospect of her wedding loomed large and real in her mind. Could she go through with sealing her vows to a man she barely knew, before friends and family, by giving him a ring?

"Of course."

Gwen's eyes shot to his face. *Of course?* What was he? Some kind of mind reader? He didn't bat an eyelid as their gazes locked. Her mouth dried as she saw the smouldering heat in his eyes—at the challenge that lay in them.

François hurried to present a tray of men's wedding rings. "Gwen, perhaps you'd like to choose for him?" he remarked as he placed the tray in front of her.

She cast her eyes over the variety of rings, some grossly ornate, others completely plain. She really didn't want to do this. It was just another symbol to mock how superficial their relationship would be. Her hand hovered over the rows of rings before she snatched one from its velvet bed. Also in platinum, and with a broad domed shape, the ring boasted a discreet diagonal curve of small, but brilliant, diamonds.

"This one'll do." She handed it to Declan.

To her discomfort, instead of taking the ring from her and trying it on, Declan put out his left hand, palm down and fingers slightly spread.

Her heart pounded in her chest and blood roared in her ears. Oh, God! She couldn't do this. Not now, not ever.

"Put it on me, Gwen." Declan's voice was soft, but there was no denying the determined order in his tone.

Taking a deep breath, and with a trembling hand, Gwen slid the ring onto his finger. There, it fit as though it had been made for him. Unbidden, a sudden and unwelcome surge of possessiveness coursed through her. A surge she rapidly quelled. What was she thinking? This was a sham. What he and Renata had had was real.

This was nothing more than a financial decision, and she'd do well to remember it.

"We'll take them both today." Declan slid the ring off his finger and gave it to François to place in a box. "Thanks, Frank. I knew you'd have what we needed. Charge it up for me. I take it you still have my details."

Declan escorted Gwen back outside. She blinked slightly in the blinding sunlight, its brightness a stark contrast to the showroom inside.

"So, where to now? Pick up my car?" she asked, hope evident in her tone.

"No. We have another appointment first, remember."

Of course, she remembered suddenly. "Connor?"

"Yeah. Those contract conditions we skirted around last night. It's time to work them out." He handed her back into the Jag. "Along with a few of my own."

Four

"So, we *have* to be married for six months for you to keep the money. Did you know that last night?" Gwen enunciated carefully from where she stood by the floor-length glass windows, her voice controlled and not letting out so much as a glimmer of the thoughts that were obviously zooming about in her head.

"Yes, I did." Declan crossed his arms and leaned back in the comfortable chair in his second, and youngest, brother Connor's office. The way she'd said it made it sound like a life sentence. He could think of worse things—but, to be honest, not many.

"And you didn't think to tell me that when we were discussing how long this…this marriage is to last?" her voice faltered slightly.

Sure he'd thought about it, but when she'd started her bartering on how long they were going to remain married he'd latched onto the idea of making the duration of their marriage her idea. She'd be less likely to back out, then, wouldn't she? A small frown creased Declan's brow and he exchanged a glance with his youngest brother, who, with a faint nod, stepped into the breach.

"Under the terms and conditions of our mother's will everything reverts to our father's trust if Declan is married for a period of less than six months." A pained expression crossed Connor's face—his thoughts on the matter quite clear. "Look, you're both rushing into this—I'm not sure you've considered all the ramifications. Why don't you take a few more days—"

"Don't worry, Connor. We wouldn't be doing this unless we absolutely had to." Lord only knew a chance like the Sellers project wouldn't come along again in a hurry. If he couldn't strike out now Cavaliere Developments would just become like one of the many subsidiary companies under the Knight Enterprises' umbrella, and that sure as hell wasn't what he wanted for the rest of his life.

Connor stepped away from his desk. "Let me explain," he offered.

"No, Connor," Declan held up a hand. "This is between the lady and me. I fight my own battles."

"Isn't that the truth," Connor muttered as he withdrew back to his desk. "Look out, world, if you ever decide to let someone else lend a hand."

Declan bit back the retort that sprung to his lips. As the eldest, he'd always assumed responsibility. Someone'd had to stand up to the old man when he and his brothers had been younger. Old habits died hard. He pushed upwards and out of his chair and strode towards the window to stand next to Gwen. Outside, the wind had picked up. Across the harbour white tips danced across the surface of the water and a large flotilla of yachts swooped, graceful and free, over the expanse of turquoise sea. How long had it been since he'd felt as free and unrestrained as the yachts on the harbour? How long since he'd done anything purely for the fun of it?

He needed to get balance back in his life—he needed to get back in control. This contract would see him home and clear. It was time to take his life back. Gwen's voice interrupted his thoughts.

"So, if we have a contract, why the need for this pre-nuptial agreement as well? After all…" she continued her voice growing heated "…it's not as if this is going to be a real marriage. You yourself called it a business arrangement last night. You know I don't want anything from you other than what we discussed." Gwen flicked a hand over towards the prenuptial agreement they'd spent the better part of the last hour arguing over, not least of which was because she'd refused to get independent legal advice on the contract.

Damn, but she was beautiful when she got angry. Hell, where had that come from? He didn't want to think of Gwen in terms of attraction. Not again.

"I don't need it for me. It's to protect you," Declan ground out through clenched teeth. He was growing mighty angry himself. He hated being this vulnerable to anyone but especially to her. He knew he should have done more to prevent her and Renata from attempting their climb that day, but Gwen could've refused to go point-blank. Where would they all be now if she had? Fate's cruel twist of irony wasn't lost on him. And despite it all, he still felt responsible for her loss, too. If he hadn't given Steve Crenshaw so much responsibility, she wouldn't be in this mess right now, either.

Gwen twisted her hands in front of her—the movement belying the rigid set of her body, the controlled rhythm of her breathing. A shaft of sunlight flashed off the diamond ring he'd bought her, reminding him of the inherent promise it held when she'd agreed to wear it. *For as long as she agreed to wear it.* What if she backed out now? A sick knot of dread tightened low in his gut. It was time to fight dirty.

"I can protect myself, you know." Her voice was low, insistent, with a husky quality that cut straight to his core and made his body react on a physical level he'd thought, after last night, he had firmly under control.

"Yeah, that much is obvious. Get real, Gwen. What are you going to do when the bank wants payment on that loan you've secured with your house? Are you just going to stand back and let them take your home?"

She flinched at the harshness of his words.

"Hey, Dec. That's a bit over the top." Connor's warning growl cut across the room.

"Over the top? No, she stands to lose as much as I do. Maybe even more. If it's going to work we both need to be fully committed." Declan turned slightly to face Gwen full on. He knew how much that house meant to her. Renata had told him about her friend's childhood, and about the maiden aunt who'd left the unencumbered property to Gwen.

Gwen's chin was down, her face slanted towards the window and her eyes were locked unblinkingly on something in the distance. He lifted her chin with one finger, forcing her to meet his gaze head-on. "What's it to be?"

She drew in a deep breath, then let it out slowly. Her face assumed a rigid cast. *Damn.* If her expression was any indicator, he'd messed up big-time.

"Give me a pen. I'll sign your damn papers—all of them." Her voice was as cold as her eyes as they stared straight back into his.

She twisted away from him and stalked back to where the papers were strewn across Connor's desk. Declan watched, his heart beating like a jackhammer against his rib cage, as she bent and signed the agreements. The soft fabric of her skirt caressed her softly rounded hips and flowed gently past her thighs.

Six months. Tension bit into his shoulders. It would be the longest six months of his life.

She was doing the right thing. She was. Gwen repeated the words in her mind over and over, as if the constant mantra would make it so. She'd been left high and dry. Any woman in her right mind would've grasped at this opportunity. It wasn't as if she was prostituting herself for the next half year, she reasoned. Not that it would come to sex, exactly. Gwen blushed as she remembered the rather explicit wording in the agreement, a copy of which lay folded neatly in the bottom of her handbag. No, intimacy was definitely not part of the bargain.

She was now bound by contract not only to be his wife but also to work for him. There was no turning back. At least she had the security of an income she was legitimately earning. She glanced over at Declan, who was attacking the prime rib-eye steak on his plate as if it was his mortal enemy. The muscles on his forearms flexed as he manipulated the knife with precision, and she stared, fascinated, at his long fingers curled around the cutlery.

An unwanted visual reminder of those same strong, tanned fingers spread across the paleness of her breasts, kneading the sensitive flesh, invaded her mind. Heat pulsed through her body, every muscle clenched in anticipation. Her fork slid from her hand to clatter noisily against her plate.

"What's the matter? Don't you like your fish?"

Gwen looked up and found herself trapped by his dark velvet eyes. "It's...it's fine, thank you." She dragged her gaze from his, and turned her attention back to her lunch. The delicately steamed John Dory had been delicious, but she'd lost all her appetite for food.

She shifted uncomfortably in her chair. She'd never survive the term of their marriage if she couldn't even sit across from him at the lunch table. Six months. It wasn't long. Not really. Certainly not the lifetime she'd expected to spend with Steve.

"You're not enjoying your meal." Declan laid his knife and fork on his near empty plate and eyed her with concern. "Would you like to leave?"

"Yes, that's probably best." Gwen bent down, grateful for the excuse not to let him see the raw hunger in her eyes, and collected her handbag from the floor as Declan called the waiter over for the bill.

"Come on, let's get you home." Declan wrapped his arm around her shoulders and coaxed her outside.

"But what about my car? We still have to collect it," Gwen protested weakly.

"Give me your keys. I'll get someone to deliver it later this afternoon."

"No, I'm fine. Honestly. I'd rather drive it home myself." Anything rather than be forced to spend another minute in close proximity with Declan Knight. She desperately needed some space, some time alone to get her thoughts back together.

He held her gently against his side, and Gwen tried to pull away and insert some distance between them.

"Appearances, remember? The society pages' editor of the paper is sitting near the back of the restaurant. She's a good friend of my father." Declan pressed hot lips against the shell of her ear, sending a thrill of anticipation shooting through her. A thrill she futilely attempted to quell. Yeah, right. Appearances. It was all about appearances. But it felt all wrong. *He* felt all wrong while, confoundingly, at the same time he felt so unbearably right.

In an attempt to bring her rebellious hormones under some semblance of control she grasped for the memory of how Steve had felt. Declan's body was firm, where Steve had been softer. He was tall, when Steve had been closer to her height. Declan's body felt hot, constantly, when—

"You look shattered. It's been a helluva day so far, huh?" Declan's deep voice vibrated through her, bringing her comparisons skidding to a halt.

"Yes, it has." In more ways than one.

"Just think, this time next week we should be getting ready for the wedding. It's at four o'clock, right?"

"Yes…four o'clock," Gwen replied distractedly. *This time next week.* The reality slammed home and doused her body's reaction to his as effectively as a bucketful of sand on a campfire.

"We'll need to correct things at the Registrar of Births, Deaths and Marriages on Monday morning," Declan continued.

"I hadn't thought of that." In fact, she was trying hard not to think about any of it.

"Connor said it'll take at least three working days before we get our license, so we'll scrape through."

Gwen wondered what Steve had done with their marriage license. Thrown it away probably, like he'd thrown away their future together. Her teeth clenched, locking her jaw. The wedding would be impossible to get through—everything as she'd meticulously planned, yet with a substitute groom. But it had to be worth it. Worth it to keep her house—the only thing she had left in her life to call her own.

Declan followed her back home after dropping her off at Libby's building to collect her car. Inside, Gwen watched as he flipped a dust cover off the sitting room sofa and sat down.

"I know you're probably sick of the sight of me, but we need to sort out a couple more things before next Saturday."

"Whatever." Gwen kept her response deliberately neutral. Sick of the sight of him? If only it could be that simple. "I'll put the kettle on first. Coffee?"

"Sure."

"I'll be back in a minute."

In the kitchen Gwen automatically put out a tray and placed on it a creamer and sugar bowl, finding respite in the automated actions. The kettle boiled all too soon and she poured the steaming water over the coffee grounds in the plunger. Two bright ceramic mugs joined the coffee carafe on the tray and she was ready to take it through to the sitting room. Gwen breathed in deeply, squared her shoulders and lifted the tray.

"Let me take that."

Gwen jumped at Declan's voice so close behind her. As he relieved her of the tray she tried to protest. "It's okay, I can manage—" But he was already walking back to the sitting room.

"When do you need to confirm numbers with the caterer?" he asked over a broad shoulder.

"By Wednesday at the latest."

"Okay, I'll make sure I let you know by then how many I'm inviting."

"The venue's only small," Gwen said, a flush of embarrassment creeping up her neck and into her cheeks. "We couldn't afford a bigger place."

"That's okay. Small suits me. But I'd like my dad and brothers there."

"Oh, sure. Of course."

"And I want you to e-mail me the schedule of costs for the wedding so I can arrange to reimburse you."

Pride insisted she argue, but pride went before a fall as she very well knew. Gwen settled for a murmur of assent instead. As Declan sat down and poured the coffee, Gwen knelt down to pick up the piece of sandpaper she'd discarded this morning, desperate for some distraction from his dominating presence.

"That would be easier with an electric sander, wouldn't it?"

"Yes, it would," she conceded through gritted teeth. How long before he'd leave her alone? "Mine's at the workshop being repaired. Besides, it's not as if I'm on a tight schedule here. I like to take my time when I can. When houses like this were built, power tools weren't invented."

Declan reached down to take one of her hands in his and turned it over, his thumbs gently stroking the calluses she'd developed over the past few years. "Do you always punish yourself like this when you try to bring things back to the way they were?"

Gwen snatched her hand away before the tingling throb

in the palm of her hand invaded her whole body. "Sometimes things are supposed to be done the hard way." *And you can take that however you darned well please.*

"Why don't you show me around? Tell me about your plans for the house."

"Why?"

"Just taking an interest in where I'll be living for the next six months."

"You? Living here?" She couldn't have heard him correctly.

"Gwen, we're getting married next week. Don't you think people would wonder why we're not living together? I know it's not what we both prefer, but if we're going to carry this off a little hardship won't do us any harm."

Hardship? He had no idea. She foolishly hadn't given a thought to where he'd live after their marriage. In fact she hadn't thought past the wedding. Gwen shook her head slowly. Her entire life had slipped out of her control.

Remember Renata. She thought again of the promise she'd made her friend. Made and yet not fulfilled. She owed her friend to see to it that Declan achieved his goal.

"Of course, you're right." She allowed a tight smile to acknowledge his point. "Okay, I'll show you the house. It won't take long. We'll start with the kitchen at the back, okay?" Maybe if they worked their way to the front door he'd take the hint and leave and she'd be rid of him. Gwen turned away, her back stiff and straight.

"Sounds good to me." Declan followed close behind. He could almost see the frustrated anger emanating off her in waves. If she held herself any more rigidly she'd probably snap. Fine tendrils of hair defied the twist she'd worn, to escape like fine threads of gossamer on her neck. If she was anyone else, he'd stop her right there in her tracks and kiss a trail across that delectable fair skin. But this was Gwen, he reminded himself grimly. No way would that be happening.

He liked what Gwen showed him in the kitchen and could plainly see how much pride she'd taken in her work. She'd be a huge asset on the Sellers project—if he got it. Once he had the old hotel converted into apartments she'd be brilliant at creating functional areas with all the automated luxuries the modern city dweller demanded, while still maintaining the age and integrity of the building's original design.

"I was lucky Aunt Hope never succumbed to the good old Kiwi do-it-yourself craze that ruined so many homes like this in the 1960s and 1970s, but she also did the bare minimum to maintain what she had. I was in my fourth year of my bachelor's degree at Victoria University when she became ill and really let the place go. She never let on how unwell she was. The next thing I knew her solicitor was calling to say the house was mine. I didn't even get a chance to attend her funeral."

"You weren't close, then?"

"You could say that." Pain shot through Gwen's chest and she pressed her lips together waiting for the pain to subside. Had it been too much for her to expect her aunt to have cherished the lost and abandoned nine-year-old who'd been deposited on her doorstep? Apparently it had. "By the time it sunk in that the house was mine to do with what I wanted, I'd already started to build a portfolio of work with clients and had a strong idea of what I wanted to do to bring the house's original beauty back. I went like a bull at a gate at first, but then as my contract commitments grew I was forced to tackle only one room at a time. Left a few others in a bit of a mess, though." Her lips pulled into a reluctant, self-deprecating smile.

"It's a big place and a heck of a lot of work for just one person. Usually you work with a crew, don't you?"

"Yes, I have my own crew of craftsmen and labourers. But not for this job." She ran a hand lovingly over a satin-finished doorframe. Her hands still intensely feminine despite the lack of manicure or softness he'd grown accustomed to in his companions. "Wherever possible, this one is for me."

"You love it, don't you? The work. The house." He couldn't take his eyes from her fingers as they stroked the polished wood. His skin stretched taut across his body, every sense standing on full alert.

She nodded, and let her hand drop from the frame, a self-conscious look chasing across her features.

"Has it always been in your family?"

"Uh-huh. Built by my great-grandfather in the late 1800s."

Declan considered her carefully. His biggest fear was that for one reason or another she'd still bail on the outrageous arrangement they'd made. But with her family heritage on the line, he had a stronger assurance. She wouldn't walk away from this in a hurry and now he felt bound to help her make sure she didn't have to. He followed her into the hallway and nodded towards a door fitted with a multicoloured stained glass panel.

"What's in here?"

"The bathroom. It was one of the first rooms I started. It's still not finished." She sighed. "But I'll get there—eventually. I have the twin of this glass window installed on the outside wall, but that's about as far as I've managed."

"Hey, don't knock yourself. It isn't as if you had enough help around the place."

"Steve did help sometimes." She was quick to rush to Crenshaw's defence, he noted, although Declan doubted the other man had been much support. From what he knew of the guy, he was more into paper solutions than physical work. Definitely not into getting his hands dirty, unless it was with someone else's money. Did she still love the jerk? he wondered. Who knew? It was irrelevant so long as she stuck to her side of the bargain.

He swung open the door, taking in the unfinished floor with ancient linoleum still adhered in places and the wallpaper that had been painted over at some time and that was now pulling away from the walls.

"You'll let me help you while I'm here?"

She looked startled. "Do I have any choice?"

Choice? No. Neither of them had any choices left. "No."

"Then why ask?"

"My mother brought me up to be polite."

A guarded look crept back in her grey eyes, darkening them to pewter. "Then I accept, since we're only being polite." Acidic tartness laced her reply.

They continued through the house, Declan asking about her plans for each room, suggesting a few ideas of his own. When they came to the bedrooms, Gwen hesitated.

"This room is mine, and—" she gestured across the hallway and two doors down, the pained expression on her face leaving him in no doubt as to her reluctance to make room for him in her home "—you can go in there—the original master bedroom. It's full of boxes at the moment but I can shift them into the old drawing room. It's my office but I don't spend a lot of time in there. A few boxes won't make much difference."

The old brass doorknob glowed a rich gold with the patina of years of use and twisted smoothly in his hand. He pushed open the door to the room she'd designated. Strips of wallpaper hung in a haphazard fashion off the walls, and threadbare carpet covered the floor.

"I'm sorry, it's not up to much. But I wasn't expecting a guest."

She did that thing with her chin again. Tilting it up as if she could take on the world. Including him. Unbidden, the need to answer her challenge rose hotly inside him. Driving his body to total awareness. Daring him to break all the rules and meet her head-on. And he would win. He'd make sure of that.

He slammed the brakes onto his wayward reaction. God, what was he thinking? This was Gwen. The one woman he should never have touched and the one woman he'd sworn he'd never touch again. Declan dragged his eyes from her face and looked around the room with a critical eye. "It's okay. If I finish stripping the walls and get rid of this carpet it should be liveable. Do you mind if I bring my own furniture?"

"Of course not. I hardly expect you to sleep on the floor."

"I'll move my things in during the week."

"You don't want to wait until after the wedding?"

"Why wait?" Declan nailed her with a dark half-lidded stare. "After the wedding everyone will expect us to take a honeymoon."

"A honeymoon? I'm *not* going on a honeymoon with you."

"Don't worry, Gwen. It's only for appearances,

remember? We don't need to go away. We'll stay here and work on the house. Together."

He watched with interest as she struggled to find an argument and was almost disappointed when her shoulders sagged and she acquiesced.

"Right. Appearances. Sure. I can live with that."

Sure she could, he thought as he drove away a few minutes later, her words still ringing in his ears. But could he? Could he live with the constant reminder of everything he'd loved and lost, all because of Gwen Jones, for the sake of his company? The answer wasn't in the fistful of spare wedding invitations scattered on the front seat of the car—thrust at him by Gwen as a last thought on his way out the door—but one thing he knew for certain. One way or another, he'd soon find out.

Five

Gwen lay face-down in a tangle of sheets, a pillow shoved over her head and her hands clamped down firmly on its feather-filled softness.

Bang. Bang. Bang.

Darn it, but the noise wouldn't go away. With a groan she pushed away the pillow to peer with bleary eyes at the pearl-white face of her alarm clock. The stark black hands finally came into focus. Seven o'clock! Who came over at seven on a Sunday morning for heaven's sake? She slid from the bed and grabbed her dressing gown from its hook behind the bedroom door. Her shoulders gave a twinge of discomfort—a reminder that she'd shifted all the heavy boxes from the spare room last night, and why.

Bang. Bang. Bang.

"Gwen? Are you okay in there?"

Declan! What on earth was he doing here already? When he'd finally left yesterday, she'd counted on his not coming around until he was ready to move his things into the spare room. She'd hoped that wouldn't be until at least Wednesday, or even later in the week.

"I'm coming!" She fumbled the key in the deadlock and swung the door wide. "What is it?" she demanded with a glare.

"You really should get a doorbell, you know." Declan grinned back, looking altogether too handsome, his long black hair loose and combed back off his face. A faded threadbare T-shirt strained at the seams across his shoulders, and equally disreputable jeans hugged his hips.

"I don't need a doorbell," Gwen instantly argued back. *I don't need you, either.* Especially not after a night of disturbing dreams that had thrust her into uncomfortable wakefulness several times before dawn.

"Not a morning person, huh?" Declan commented cheerfully as he gently shouldered past her, carrying a large toolkit under one arm and a neatly folded tarpaulin in his other hand.

"Humph!" Gwen wheeled around and stalked back to her bedroom. *Slam!* Her door rattled on its hinges and she bit back a groan when she saw the crack appear in the plasterboard around the doorframe.

Blast him! Now look what he's made me do! she thought angrily.

She flopped onto her bed and pulled the covers back over her. Morning person, indeed. She heard him moving about in the hallway as he made several trips out to the car and back again. Finally the front door swung shut and then there was nothing but blessed silence. Her eyelids drifted closed.

An enticing scent tweaked at her nostrils and dragged her from sleep. Coffee? A half-opened eye showed the hands of her alarm had swung around to ten o'clock. *Ten o'clock!* Gwen shot instantly awake and flew across the room to pull open her door.

The sinfully fragrant aroma of freshly perked coffee floated down the hallway from the kitchen. A clatter, followed swiftly by a muffled curse, sounded from Declan's bedroom. She halted in the open doorway. Low makeshift scaffolding had been erected along one wall and he'd obviously worked hard for the past three hours. Hard and hot, by the looks of him. He'd discarded the T-shirt.

Gwen tried to ignore the heavy swell of desire that tautened her skin and caused a throb deep within her as she took in the planes of his broad muscled back and followed the line of his spine until it disappeared beneath his low-slung waistband. His skin glistened with exertion. He'd tied his hair back off his face with a thin strip of leather and wielded a steam gun in one hand and a scraper in the other to ease away the last of the wallpaper from where it clung with tenacious determination.

She swallowed to moisten her throat. "Having fun?"

The muscles across the top of his shoulders tightened at her words, his only acknowledgement of her presence. Eventually, his task complete as the final strip of paper fell to the floor, Declan turned to face her.

"You're awake at last." He put down his tools and pulled a disreputable-looking towel from where he'd tucked it into his waistband. Without the extra bulk of the fabric his denims slid down a notch, exposing another couple of inches of tanned skin and with them the shadowed lines of his hips. "Hungry?"

An escalating curl of warmth spiralled through her belly as she forced herself to tear her gaze from the hidden promise of what lay beneath his jeans. Her breasts swelled and tightened, her nipples pressing achingly against the sheer fabric of her nightgown and robe.

What had he said? Hungry. Yes. No! For food. Only food, she reminded herself with a hard mental shake. She dragged her eyes upwards until they locked with the heat reflected in his. He knew, darn him. He knew exactly what kind of effect he had on her.

"You could pour us a cup of that coffee." His eyes remained fixed on hers, unblinking. All seeing.

"Sure. I'll get the coffee." Gwen fled down the hallway, grateful for an excuse to avoid looking at him. To avoid acknowledging her instant, weak reaction.

It was the dreams. Stupid, stupid dreams. Although their shadowed content had escaped her waking mind, the tightly coiled sense of frustration lingered. Any woman with blood in her veins would have reacted to Declan like that when forced to come face-to-face with his blatant masculinity again, she desperately rationalised. Her stomach clenched at the memory.

"I'll have mine black." He sauntered into the kitchen and leaned one hip against the countertop. Gwen thanked her lucky stars he'd put his shirt back on. "Sleep well?"

She sloshed coffee from the carafe into a mug and pushed it over to him. "Yes, thank you."

She poured another mug for herself and added a liberal measure of milk before lifting the warm brew to her lips.

"Ohhhhh." She sighed. "This is good." It definitely wasn't her regular brand. Nothing she'd bought had ever tasted this sinfully divine.

"It's one of Mason's special blends. I brought a few things over from his place this morning."

Gwen took another deep swallow of the coffee and savoured the full flavour as it rolled across her tongue. Suddenly mindful of the way Declan watched her she put her mug back down onto the bench and grabbed a couple of slices of bread to pop into her toaster.

"Have you eaten?" she asked, making herself busy collecting spread from the refrigerator and opening the pantry door in an attempt to put a physical barrier between them.

"Yeah, hours ago. I brought you a present, by the way." Declan put down his mug and turned to lift a brown-paper-wrapped box from one of the bentwood kitchen chairs. He placed it on the kitchen table.

"A present? Whatever for?" Gwen eyed it warily.

"Call it an early wedding present."

"I don't want a wedding present." *From you.*

"Go on. Open it."

"Really, Declan. I don't want a wedding present."

"Okay, call it a contribution to household expenses then. I can pay those, remember?" Some of the friendly light in his eyes dimmed as he reminded her of the contract they'd argued about. Was it only yesterday? "I'd better get back to work." Without waiting to see if she opened the present or not, he topped up his coffee and left her alone.

The toaster popped up, giving her the perfect excuse to ignore the parcel for a while longer. With her toast buttered and spread with marmalade, Gwen took her coffee and plate over to the kitchen table and sat down. She stared idly outside. Some of the roses needed dead-heading and the weeds had sprung back with a vengeance. There was always something to do around here. Maybe she'd work outside today, enjoy the sunshine outdoors. Be anywhere on the property Declan wasn't.

Her eyes flicked back to the box. Neither its shape nor its size gave any clue as to the contents. What on earth had he bought?

She wasn't interested. Not a bit. Gwen took another bite of her toast and looked once more at the box. A piece of tape at one end had lifted. She allowed her fingernail to play at it, loosening it further until a flap of paper was free. Feminine curiosity eventually got the better of her and she pulled at the remaining tape until the wrapper fell away to expose the box.

A sander! He'd bought her a top-of-the-range electric sander, with attachments that made her old one look like it had been used in the construction of the ark. A small note was taped to the lid of the box. *"To protect your hands."* Gwen emptied the box of its contents and laid each piece out on the tabletop. Tucked in at the side, near the bottom, was another wrapped package—this one cylindrical in shape. The note on the side said, *"To repair the damage you've already done."*

Puzzled, Gwen ripped away the paper to find a tube of aloe-based hand cream, rich with pure essential oils to repair and nourish damaged skin. She undid the lid and breathed in the scent. It smelled blissful. A tiny bit of cream oozed from the top and she rubbed it into the back of her hand.

A sigh of regret floated past her lips as she gazed at the sander on the tabletop. She couldn't accept it.

"Like it?" Declan loomed in the doorway.

"You know I can't accept this."

"Why not?" His words were sharp and his dark

eyebrows drew together in a straight line she was coming to recognise as suppressed irritation. Being told 'no' obviously didn't sit well with Declan Knight.

"Well…" she faltered.

"Looks like it's yours, then."

"Declan—"

"Gwen, get used to it. For the next six months I'm going to be a part of your life—and, for what it's worth, you're going to be a part of mine. Maybe you don't understand what getting this trust fund means to me but believe me, the cost of that sander is nothing, *absolutely nothing,* compared to what I will gain in the long run."

"Couldn't you have bought a less expensive model?"

"Of course I could've. But why would I? Call it your spare. Call it anything. It doesn't matter much to me either way."

Gwen couldn't think of a suitable answer. She put out a hand to touch the machine again. She was being a stubborn, prideful fool.

"Thank you," she murmured as she turned in her chair, but he'd gone again.

She heard him down the hallway, first shifting the scaffolding, then gathering the strips of sodden paper and stuffing them into a rubbish sack with a fervour she knew was her fault. This was going to be harder than she imagined. Much, much harder.

It had taken him the better part of the day, but the walls were ready to be sized. Until Gwen was ready to decorate this room he had a couple of colourful hand-knotted rugs he'd collected on his overseas travels that he could hang for some colour.

He'd barely seen Gwen. Still, that was probably a good thing, considering she'd only been in her night-gown and robe for most of the morning. An unbidden flare of desire arced through his body.

He'd been grateful for something physical to distract him while she'd slept or he may have felt tempted to join her. Damn, but this was getting tricky. What had seemed the perfect solution on Friday night had turned into a web of complications he hadn't foreseen.

If anyone had told him a week ago that Gwen Jones would be boiling his blood he'd have laughed out loud. He'd sworn off her the minute he'd dragged himself to his senses the morning after Renata's funeral. The morning after he'd lost himself, and all sense, in the soft curves of Gwen's giving body.

His body leaped to fiery attention at the memory of the silken softness of her skin, of her legs tangled in his, of the surprising strength in her arms as she'd held him to her and of the hunger of her kiss. The memory was both exhilarating and crucifying at the same time, and he still hadn't figured out how to deal with the aftermath. Even after all this time he still hadn't purged her from his memory, and his body let him know it.

Disgusted with himself, Declan set to packing up his tools and clearing the last of the rubbish as if his sanity depended on it. A rusty laugh echoed in the empty room. Yeah, maybe it did after all. He had to be mad to have put himself in this whole situation.

The clearing up finally done, he rotated his shoulders to work out the knots he'd developed while scraping constantly at the years' worth of accumulated layers of wallpaper and let go a sigh of satisfaction. It was good to be on the tools—it was still the side of his job he loved the most. Tools. He frowned. She hadn't wanted to accept the sander from him. It was too bad. She was going to have to get used to it, and him.

Absently, he picked a scrap of sticky paper from his shirt. He could do with a hot shower, or a good rubdown. Or both. He grimaced at his ridiculous thoughts. Like he'd stand a chance at both here with Gwen.

"You're finished?" Gwen stood poised in the doorway. She'd changed her nightgown for a pair of denim cut-offs and a short-sleeved blouse that she'd knotted at her waist. A floppy brimmed straw hat was perched on her head and judging by the faint bloom of colour on her skin she'd been working outside.

"Yeah. Where can I put the rubbish?"

"Here, let me take it." She stepped forward into the room and reached to take the bag from him.

"No, it's okay. Just tell me where to put it," he insisted.

Gwen didn't let go. He gave the bag a tug. "Does everything have to be a battle with you?"

She uncurled her fingers from the bag one by one. "Down the side of the house will do fine. You'll see where when you get outside." Her voice was stiff, like the set of her shoulders.

With his free hand Declan grabbed her wrist, turning her hand palm down. "Where's your ring?" he scowled.

"In its case. I've been working in the garden."

"You don't wear gloves?" It was obvious by the dirt under her nails that she hadn't.

"Do *you?*" she fired back quickly before snatching her hand back. "Don't think because we're engaged you can order me about. You don't call all the shots."

"I was thinking of your hands. For the wedding photos."

"Oh." Gwen curled her fingers and examined them closely. "Don't worry, I'll make sure they're clean."

Declan let go of the rubbish sack and took her hand again, examining it closely as she had. He rubbed his thumb across the backs of her fingers as he assessed the damage she'd wrought today.

"Yeah, you do that." He dropped her hand like a hot potato, snagged the bag in one fist and stalked up the hallway to dump the rubbish outside. He shouldn't let her get under his skin like that, but somehow, it was easier said than done.

Gwen jumped as the front door slammed. All she'd been going to do was offer him a meal. He'd eaten the sandwiches she shoved through his doorway at lunchtime, but a man his size was bound to be hungry now. It was coming up six o'clock. She looked around the room. It would have taken her a week to get all that paper off. He'd done it in a day, and properly, too.

"I'll have my things sent around tomorrow," he said from behind her.

Gwen jumped. "Couldn't you whistle or something when you're coming!" How often was he going to sneak up on her like that?

"What, like this?" Declan pursed his lips and gave a long, low wolf-whistle.

"On second thought, don't bother." Gwen couldn't stop the blush that spread up her neck and flamed her cheeks. "I'll get used to you."

"You'd better." Declan bent to pick up the toolkit and started to refold the tarpaulin he'd spread across the floor. "I'll go and put these in the car and then I'll be on my way."

"I...um." Sudden nerves churned in her stomach. What the hell was she doing? She didn't want to spend any more time with him than absolutely necessary yet here she was trying to ask him to stay for dinner?

"You um what?" His voice was clipped, as if he'd had enough of her and her company.

"I took some steaks from the freezer a couple of hours ago. I wondered if you'd like dinner before you go."

He hesitated for a moment before replying. "I'm a bit on the ripe side. Is there any chance I could have a shower? I have a change of clothes in the car."

"The shower's not installed yet, but you can have a bath if you'd like."

She wondered what he'd make of that. A bath. Granted, the deep, claw-footed tub in her decrepit bathroom was larger than the standard bath of today, but then Declan Knight was larger than the standard man, too.

"I don't suppose there's any chance it's a spa?" He arched a thick black eyebrow in hopeful query.

"Not a chance." Gwen grinned back.

"Well, it looks like it's a bath then. Give me a couple of minutes to get my things together."

Gwen was running the taps and taking the largest fluffy towel she could find from the cupboard when Declan came into the bathroom.

"I put some bath salts in there for you. I know how my shoulders feel after all that kind of work. It'll help ease the knots out."

"Thanks." Declan lifted his T-shirt up over his head.

"Excuse me." Gwen bolted for the door.

"What's the matter? It's not like you haven't seen me half-naked before."

Or completely naked, Gwen remembered with another rush of heat to her cheeks. "I thought I'd give you a bit of privacy."

Behind her she heard the rasp of the zipper of his jeans before the dull thud of fabric on the floor. Don't turn around. *Don't turn around.*

She turned around.

He bent to test the water and that was enough for her. She was out of there like an Olympic sprinter off the blocks. The faint rumble of his laughter penetrated the door as she pulled it closed behind her.

Garlic pepper steak. No, double chilli garlic pepper steak. It was the only suitable revenge she could think of. But she couldn't help but hesitate and rest her head against the door long enough to hear his deep sigh of satisfaction and the gentle lap of water against the sides of the tub as he sank into the bath.

What was she thinking? Next she'd be plastering her eye to the keyhole to take a peek. Gwen mentally revised her renovation plans to include having the shower installed as soon as possible. Once they had the Sellers contract and her progress contract payments started coming in it would be first on her list, no matter what else may have taken top priority for work around here. She'd even take a part-time job at the local takeaway bar if she had to.

Anything would be better than imagining him in her tub every night.

Anything.

Six

The scents of sandalwood and lavender wafted past her nose as Gwen straightened the duvet over the king-sized sleigh bed that had been delivered earlier today and now silently dominated the old master bedroom. How did he get his linen to smell like that? She flicked the corners of the pillows one last time. There, that looked better.

At the end of the bed she trailed her hand along the edge of the footboard and tried to ignore the expanse of fine cotton that encased the wickedly plush feather duvet. The bed looked new, but she wondered if he had slept in it before. Slept in it with someone else.

She tried not to imagine his long dark hair spread in wild abandon over the rich, ruby-coloured pillows, or his tanned skin against the dusky sheets. A tiny moan slipped past her lips at the sudden, intensely vivid image that flooded her mind.

She locked her knees rigidly straight and desperately gathered her wild imagination back under control. No intimacy. No repeat of the mistakes of the past. Gwen forced her wayward thoughts into submission just as she heard a key in the front door and a measured tread down the hall.

He was home.

Home? When on earth did she start thinking of Declan and home in the same sentence? That implied a permanence she was never going to have. Not with him, anyway.

"You didn't need to go to the bother of making up the bed, I'd have done that."

Gwen congratulated herself silently. She didn't so much as flinch this time as he appeared beside her.

"I know, but when you called to say you were working late I thought I'd help out. I've kept you some dinner. It's in the oven."

"Thanks, I appreciate it." Declan tossed his briefcase on the bed and flipped it open. "Here, I brought something for you in case you want to get started on the job before the wedding."

Gwen reached for the DVD case he held out. "A disk?"

"Yeah, I had the chance to go through the hotel today and took some video. I thought you might like to view it—you know, start putting some thoughts together, see what you could be letting yourself in for."

Excitement thrilled through her. She loved the planning stage of every job. Being able to visualise what she had to do, to put each thing in its place and start sourcing the appropriate fittings and furniture, was the best part of her job. Declan threw another packet onto the bed. Celluloid images—some colour, some black and white—spilled out to scatter over the bedcovers.

"These are from around the time the hotel closed for guests and date back to when the hotel originally opened."

Gwen sat down on the bed and snatched up the photos, eager to see the images. She flipped past the current photos quickly, lingering when she reached the older ones. "These are amazing. Do you know if they've kept any of the original furnishings or light fittings?"

"There are a few, especially in the hotel lobby and restaurant, and I understand there's a massive storage area in the hotel basement, too."

"Do you think I could take a look sometime?"

"There's an inventory in the paperwork I requested. That'll do for now. Once we get the job you can hunt and pick as much as you like."

Gwen tried to hide her disappointment, but what he said made sense. No point getting her hopes up or getting all excited when they might not even get the job. And if they didn't? What then? What of the wedding they had looming ahead of them at the end of the week. Would it all be in vain?

"It'll be okay, Gwen. No one else has our combined experience. We *will* get this job."

He was too astute. It wasn't fair that he could read her so well.

"Yeah, I know. I just can't help worrying." Gwen's voice caught in her throat. She knew all too well how easily hopes and dreams could be ripped apart. How a life, so perfect in every way, could be destroyed in a careless moment. Had she become some kind of Jonah that everything she'd held dear in her life had been laid to waste—first, her parents' marriage, then her mother's desertion of her, then Steve? And worse, Renata?

"Hey, don't worry." Declan sat down on the bed next to her. "It'll be okay, you'll see."

Gwen allowed herself to draw strength from the assurance in his voice. If only she could rest her cheek against his broad shoulder, lean into him and absorb his comfort. She drew in a deep breath, steeling herself against giving in to the weakness that urged her to seek comfort in his arms, to inhale the scent she'd long since come to associate only with him. Her heart hammered in her chest. It would be so simple to just let go, to turn into him and—

Declan got up from the bed, the movement throwing Gwen slightly off balance and bringing her rampaging thoughts back under control. Just as well.

He shrugged out of his suit jacket and slipped his vibrant silk tie loose at his neck before unhooking the top two buttons of his shirt with a sound of relief that bordered on a growl.

"Tough day?" Gwen asked, then wished the words unsaid. Well, wasn't she slipping into the little wife mode already.

"Yeah, board meeting. I had to bring the board members up to date with the police investigation. It wasn't pretty." Declan slung his jacket on the bed and hooked a T-shirt and jeans from the chest of drawers that was wedged under the window on the other side of the room. The late afternoon sun streamed in through the window, gilding him as he stood framed by golden beams of light. He sighed. "And then I told them about the wedding and the tender for the Sellers Hotel."

"How did your dad take the news?"

Declan's short bark of laughter fractured the air between them. "As well as could be expected." His lips pressed together in a grim line. "He doesn't like having his plans upset. His vision for Cavaliere Developments runs along a different line to mine."

Gwen frowned. "It's hellish being at cross purposes like that." A memory flashed through her mind of Aunt Hope's stern and unforgiving face as she greeted nine-year-old Gwen when, after her mother's latest beau had objected to Gwen's presence on his luxury yacht, she'd arrived in New Zealand—alone, totally confused and rejected even by the man she'd been brought up to believe was her father. The whole time she'd lived with Aunt Hope she'd been filled with stories of her mother's failures—failure to maintain a successful career, failure to maintain a successful relationship, failure to be a good mother. Failures Gwen refused to replicate.

"It has its moments." Declan's comment dragged her back to the present. He sat back down onto the bed and looked at Gwen. "He's definitely coming to the wedding—are you okay about that?"

"Shouldn't I be?" He'd already told her he wanted his family there. It wasn't as if she could object, anyway. Even so, the prospect of meeting Declan's father did set her stomach aflutter. He was the kind of man whose reputation as a tough negotiator preceded him in foot-high letters. No one fooled Tony Knight.

Declan kicked off his shoes and they landed with a dull thud on the bare floor. "He might ask you a few questions, that's all."

"What sort of questions?"

"Where we met, how long ago. That sort of thing."

Gwen chewed on her lower lip. There were bound to be quite a few of those sorts of questions floating around next Saturday.

"It's not as if we were strangers. We can easily tell

him the truth—that we met eight-and-a-half years ago but haven't seen much of one another until recently." The instant the words were out of her mouth she wished them unsaid. Renata had introduced them, filled with the excitement of a prospective bride and insisting her two best friends get along.

For Gwen it had been a bitter pleasure-pain to meet Declan Knight. From the first time she'd shook his hand in greeting she'd felt a trickle of sexual awareness. An awareness she'd spent the better part of the next six months valiantly ignoring, until that fateful night when commonsense, relegated to the backseat by grief, had let her down and she'd acted purely on instinct. Instinct that had seen her burned so badly she'd promised she'd never let herself feel so much, so deeply, for a man ever again.

Gwen rapidly gathered her thoughts into some semblance of order as facts slotted back into place. "Declan, it's simple. We met through Renata." She turned away from the sudden pain she saw reflected in Declan's eyes and the tightness that bracketed his lips as he clenched his jaw. "Then, more recently we've seen each other off and on through work. It's all true, surely we don't need to go into too much detail—oh no!"

"What?"

"The invitations I gave you. They had Steve's name on them."

"I noticed," Declan replied wryly. "Don't worry, I had my secretary scan them up and change the minor details before reprinting them."

Minor details. Gwen clenched her hands into fists so tight her fingernails bit painfully into the palms of her hands. Minor details like the groom being a different man? Minor details like how false this entire wedding was going to be? Minor details like the lie she was going to live for the next six months so she could be certain her home would be safe?

"I'll leave you to get changed." Her voice was strained.

Declan gently grabbed her arm before she left.

"Gwen. It's going to be okay. I won't let you lose this place, whatever happens."

She flicked a glance at his face. His eyebrows were pulled together, his dark eyes burned with concern and a tiny frown marred the perfection of his forehead. Gwen clamped down on the urge to smooth away the creases. Clamped down hard.

"Thanks, I know, I'll be fine." She stiffened and pulled away, closing the door gently behind her.

Declan watched her go, frustration building inside of him at the way she would bend, almost break, and then in an instant be as strong as a reed in the wind. Bowing but never giving in. She did it all the time. Assumed responsibility. Bore it alone on her slender shoulders. What had made her like that, he wondered?

Had it been when Renata died that day on the mountain, or did it go back further? He knew she still blamed herself—heaven knew he did, too, in so many ways. But even so, *he* was the one who should have been there with both of them, but he'd been too damned busy with his fledgling business to take a day out to go climbing with them. Sharp pain burst in his chest as he remembered them heading out that day. One, daylight and energy—the other, moonlight and secrets. Each the antithesis of the other, yet despite their disparity they'd been the best of friends.

The next time he'd seen them he'd been part of the rescue team sent to pluck Gwen from the ledge that had saved her. They hadn't let him be part of the crew that had retrieved Renata's body, no matter how much he'd insisted. But he'd been there when they'd brought her down the mountain.

He groaned and pushed the thought far, far into the recesses of his mind. Down that road lay only torment—torment he already had a painfully intimate relationship with. He stripped off his shirt, balling it up before tossing it into the corner with a curse. He had more problems on his hands than what had happened in the past and what made Gwen Jones tick.

His father wasn't happy. Not happy at all. Somehow, in the next five days, Declan had to convince Gwen to be an ardent loving bride or, with a full complement of legal might behind him, his father would usurp his plans.

He dropped backwards onto the bed and lay staring at the painted kauri-batten ceiling. He could hear Gwen moving about in her workroom-cum-office next door, and the occasional floorboard would creak as she paced from one side of the room to the other.

His eyes slid shut and he tried to visualise her. She probably was poring over those photos and the video already. Bit by bit, muscle by muscle, he felt the tight, coiled tension that had seen him through the day begin to ease off. A small, satisfied smile crept across his face. At least he'd done something right by bringing those pictures home. The light of enthusiasm in her face had been like a gift.

He sighed and levered himself up off the bed, a rueful expression on his face as he saw the crumpled bed linen. His mother would have skinned him for lying on the freshly made bed. He wondered how

Gwen felt about it. Despite living in a house in a constant state of chaos through the renovation she kept things very tidy.

Would it bother her? No, she probably wouldn't care. But out of habit, Declan quickly smoothed over the damage before changing his clothes and hanging his suit in the freestanding wardrobe perched in the corner of the room. Funny, that hadn't been here when he'd left last night. Gwen must have manoeuvred it in on her own after he'd gone.

He opened the door and a whiff of her gentle fragrance escaped. If he wasn't mistaken, this was her wardrobe. It looked like she was pulling out all the stops for him.

But would she agree to his next request?

For the moment, Gwen had abandoned the hotel project in favour of her own. The brush she was using to work the paint stripper into the carvings on the mantelpiece dangled, redundant, from her gloved fingers when Declan sauntered into the sitting room.

From her vantage point on the floor she was in the perfect position to eye his long legs encased in worn denim that hugged every part of him as if it had been custom made for his body. *Every* part of him. Her heart stuttered against the wall of her chest.

"Your dinner will be dried out by now," she pointed out, forcing her heartbeat to a normal rhythm through sheer will. If she could only get him to leave the room she'd be fine.

"It'll be all right."

Gwen rose to her feet and pulled off the gloves she wore more as a concession to Declan's not so subtle remarks about the condition of her hands than the characteristics of the paint stripper. "I'll get it for you."

"You don't need to wait on me, Gwen. I can get it myself. I need to ask you something before I eat, though."

His tone was serious and Gwen's stomach sank. What did he want now? He'd taken over her home and her life. Was there anything left?

"What is it?" she sighed as she sat down on the dustcover protecting the couch. Somehow she was certain that whatever he was going to say to her, she would be best sitting down.

"We have to be lovers."

"We *what?*" Gwen shot to her feet. "No way. That's so not part of the deal." She crossed her arms firmly in front of her. She had to or she'd probably throw something at him, starting with the pot of paint stripper she'd been using. "If you'll remember, we've been there and done that. It didn't work then, it sure as hell won't work now," she growled.

"Hell, that didn't come out right." An aggravated look of disgust crossed Declan's face.

"You can bet your life it didn't. And you can bet your life it isn't going to happen this side of hell freezing over, either."

"That's not what I meant. Sit down."

"I'd prefer to stand at the moment, thank you." Gwen bristled.

"I'll start again—"

"You can start as many times as you like, it isn't going to change my mind." Gwen marched over to the sash window to stare blindly through the glass, counting to ten several times over while she tried to calm down.

"Don't go getting all twisted up about it. I made a

mistake, okay? And before you jump down my throat again and say 'too right,' you've got the wrong end of the stick."

Gwen turned and narrowed wary eyes at him. "So what is it, then?"

"Do you remember what I said about how my father was probably going to ask questions?"

Gwen nodded.

"He's expecting to see a devoted couple."

Gwen froze on the spot. She had a very bad feeling about where this was heading. "How devoted?"

"Totally." Declan bent his head and rubbed one hand across the back of his neck. "He's expecting the real deal and if he doesn't see what he's expecting, Connor's warned me I'm going to have a massive legal wrangle over my eligibility to benefit from the trust fund."

"But your mother's will said you only have to be married, doesn't it? Surely it didn't specify love ever after." Gwen spat the last words. They'd left a very nasty taste in her mouth.

She'd seen the harm foolish dreams of forever wreaked when her mother's infidelity destroyed her parents' marriage and along with that Gwen's entire world when the only father she'd known had found out she wasn't his biological child. Love, in her world, was not an ever-after option.

"Dad is one of the trustees. He's going to fight me on this unless we can convince him it's a love match."

Gwen tried to ignore the churning in her stomach. "Convince him it's a love match? No, I can't do it."

"Look, it's only for the day. He's flying out for meetings in the States straight after the reception. In fact, we're lucky he's so busy preparing for his trip or he'd have insisted on having us over for dinner this week. Please, Gwen, this is really important."

"Of course it's important, to you. You get to control your precious company," she retaliated.

"Well, let's not forget what you get in all this. It's not like you're doing it out of the love of your heart."

His words split apart the air between them as effectively as if a shard of ice had suddenly lodged painfully between her ribs, robbing her of breath and sending a chill deep into her chest. He'd dealt his trump card, and he knew it. She'd do anything to keep the house. Anything. If that meant being Declan's radiant, *devoted* bride, she had to agree.

She forced her assent past the mass that had lodged in her throat. "Okay, I'll do it." Her voice reduced to a whisper.

"We'd better get some practice in, then."

With one swift step he was in front of her and had bent his head to lower his lips to hers. Gwen felt their heated pressure before her mind assimilated his intention. Her lips parted on a shocked gasp and he caught her lower lip gently between his own, pulling softly, coaxing her to respond.

A sudden powerful wave of desire, sweet and sharp, caught her off guard and undulated from the soles of her feet, rocking her against him. She splayed her fingers across the hard muscles of his chest, feeling them flex beneath her hands as he drew in a shallow breath. Declan deepened the kiss, robbing her of sensibility. As effectively as he'd invaded her home, now he invaded her sanity and, as she gave herself over to sensation, she accepted she was powerless to stop him.

Her hands roamed across his chest and over his

shoulders until they looped across the back of his neck. His hair was loose and felt like raw silk against her fingers, while his lips were like velvet against hers. She kissed him back with a need she'd kept under lock and key for eight long years. Impenetrable by anyone but Declan Knight. A need she'd never wanted to experience again.

This was what it had been like—an all-consuming craving for more—except she didn't want to recognise this intense desire in herself—this absolute hunger. Needs she'd believed could remain in slumberous oblivion. Needs she'd told herself she could live without.

Declan's mouth burned a hungry trail across her cheek and along her jaw. His lips captured her ear lobe and drew it into the warmth of his mouth. A tiny cry of surprise jolted her into awareness. What the heck was she doing? She yanked herself from his arms, forcing him to let her go. Her breathing was ragged, speech impossible. Declan spun away from her. His breathing none too steady either. But then he turned and trapped her with a searing look. A look with eyes still aflame with desire. Desire for *her*.

His voice, once he'd harnessed the control required to speak, was deep, guttural. "If we can carry that off, it should be convincing enough, don't you think?"

"You have no idea," she whispered harshly. She turned and fled the room before he could catch a glimpse of the tears that suddenly shimmered in her eyes.

That night Gwen lay rigid in her bed. The sheets were barely disturbed. Across the hall she imagined she could make out the steady, deep breathing that indicated Declan, at least, was asleep.

Of course he was, he had the promise of what he needed, and somehow she was going to have to find the strength to provide it.

Seven

Gwen woke to the sounds of Declan moving about in her kitchen. She touched her fingers to her lips, recalling the feel and even the taste of him from last night. She groaned and rolled over onto her stomach, thumping the pillow with fisted hands. Damn Declan for kissing her, and damn her for enjoying it.

A knock at her bedroom door only slightly preceded the creak of hinges as the door opened and the object of her thoughts, suited up and ready for work, entered carrying a tray.

"Breakfast," he said as he brought the tray over to her. "We need to talk."

She didn't like the way this was headed. The last time he'd said that, look what had happened? At the memory, her body responded with its own ripple of arousal, beading her nipples to tight peaks against the soft fabric of her nightgown. She yanked the covers up and tucked her arms tightly over them to hide the incriminating effect he had on her.

Declan's dark eyes were dull, fogged with weariness, and tiny lines bracketed his lips. So he hadn't had such a great night after all. A triumphant flare of satisfaction ignited and equally as quickly extinguished as Gwen recalled her own troubled sleep. At this rate they'd both be wrecks by Saturday. He was right. They did have to talk.

"I'm sorry I surprised you last night," he started as he handed her a mug of tea and offered her the small creamer and sugar pot on the tray.

Gwen added a dash of milk and shook her head at the sugar. "Surprised? You made me angry, too."

"I know. I didn't mean to make you angry. To be honest that kiss wasn't what I was expecting, either."

What had he been expecting? she wondered. She wrapped nerveless fingers around the warm mug. Better not to know. "Where do we go from here?" she asked.

The shrill buzz of Declan's cell phone interrupted whatever he was going to say. "Excuse me a minute," he said as he flipped the phone open. Whatever the news, it wasn't good, judging by the expression on his face. With a sharp, "I'll get back to you," he slapped the phone shut and shoved it back in his pocket.

"Bad news?" Gwen asked.

"Yeah, unfortunately, I have to go. Some vandalism on one of the jobs we're working on. I doubt I'll have this sorted before late tonight. Do you mind?"

"Why should I mind?" She went for the couldn't-care-less approach. The less he realised how last night's kiss had jeopardised her control the better. Discussing it would only prolong the agony.

"We'll talk later, okay?" He was already on his way out the door.

"Don't worry. Later will be fine. There's no rush." Gwen selected a triangle of toast from the tray with a nonchalance she was far from feeling. "Thanks for the breakfast."

Declan fired a quick, heart-stopping grin at her. "We *are* going to sort this out you know." He disappeared from the doorway and she heard him grab his briefcase from his room before heading towards the front door.

She sagged against her pillows in relief as she heard the front door close, then the sound of his Jaguar starting up. He was gone. Reprieve.

The house had an empty, hollow feel to it when Gwen arrived back from a long afternoon doing lunch and shopping with Libby. It was late. The sun had dropped behind the horizon in a fireball of colour and the grey light of dusk now shrouded the house. From the lack of vehicle out front and the hollow emptiness inside, Declan wasn't home yet. Strange how she'd never noticed how large and echoing the house was before. It was as if he'd expanded somehow to fill it with his presence, as if he belonged there.

Don't be stupid. She shook her head at her fanciful imaginings. *You've had too much wine with lunch.* She dropped her handbag and coat on her bed and slipped her feet out of the high-heeled court shoes she'd worn to match the sleek watermelon-coloured sheath that had armoured her for her afternoon with Libby. Surprisingly, Libby had accepted the sudden change in wedding plans without demur. Maybe it'd been because she was so high on the buzz of excitement she'd shown when seeing Gwen's engagement ring for the first time, or the fact she'd never really warmed to Steve in the first place.

Gwen was glad she'd decided to spend the time with Libby, but while the mental exertion required to maintain the blushing bride façade had been good practice for Saturday, it had been exhausting. At least they'd managed to have their last meeting with the florist about table settings at the reception and had picked up the dresses from the dressmaker.

Her cheeks ached from the perpetual smile she'd kept plastered to her face as Libby had made her try on the soft white A-line gown and had enthused again about the pearl-beaded lace empire-style bodice. It was hard to believe she'd once quietly been as excited as her friend over the elegant design. But that seemed like a lifetime ago.

Gwen padded on bare feet down the hall to the bathroom. A long, relaxing soak in the bath was what she needed. She flipped open the taps and poured in a handful of bath crystals, flinching as she remembered doing the same thing for Declan only a few days ago. Heavens, she couldn't even take a bath now without him muscling in on it.

She wondered how his day had gone. Vandalism and theft were major problems on construction sites. Clearly things weren't going brilliantly, or he'd have been back by now. Back to continue the discussion they'd been forced to abandon this morning.

Gwen slid the side-opening zipper down on her dress and peeled the garment off her. She bent to swirl the bath water with a lazy hand, inhaling deeply the calming aroma of the jasmine-scented bath crystals. Not in the mood for the harsh overhead light, she decided to light the candles she had in various shapes and sizes on the antique vanity unit. *Oh yes, that was much better.* With the muted light reflected in the slightly tarnished mirror she could feel her cares diminish already—well, almost.

She swiftly stripped off her lacy underwear, twisted her hair up into a clip on top of her head, and stepped into the bath. *Ah, bliss.* Inch by inch her body sank into the water. She toed the taps shut and lay back and closed her eyes, revelling in the peace and silence.

Declan rolled his car to a halt in Gwen's driveway and turned off the motor. Lord, he was tired. Nothing, but nothing, had gone right today. He had his suspicions about who was responsible for the vandalism of the imported timber he'd paid an arm and a leg to bring in for this job, but convincing the officers in charge of the investigation was going to be another matter entirely.

And then there was Gwen.

Unbidden the memory of their kiss last night deluged his senses, tightening his muscles and flooding him with heat. He certainly hadn't expected that kind of reaction, either from him or her. He could still see her eyes as she'd stared at him accusingly before taking flight from the room last night, every bit as much want reflected in their smoky depths as had pounded through his body.

No physical intimacy. He'd reminded himself of that constantly last night while he'd cleaned up the paint stripper she'd abandoned. Abandoned because he'd breached the terms of their agreement.

He really had thought it would be no problem to adhere to that particular rule, but suddenly his body was urging him to trash the agreement and draw up a new one. One that gave them full rights to explore the potential he knew lay between them. His lips curled in an ironic twist. Yeah, and Gwen would agree to that some time—like never.

Declan refused to admit that this time he'd been too ambitious or that his father might have been right. There was more to life than pedantic, predictable plodding. Sometimes you had to stick out your neck—take risks. And he knew where he was going to start tonight. With Gwen.

He let himself quietly into the house. Had she gone to bed already? No, it wasn't that late, only eight o'clock. His eye caught the flicker of light from the bathroom. He sniffed the air suspiciously, his nostrils identifying the mixed aromas of candle wax and a wickedly sweet floral scent that reminded him completely of Gwen and that wreaked havoc with his libido. The muted drip of water into the deep bath filtered down the hall.

A vision of her, in the water, her soft creamy skin bathed in a golden glow of light, painted itself behind his eyes and arousal ripped at him with sudden, sharp claws. Every nerve ending screamed at him to stalk down that hallway and lift her, warm and wet, from the water and take her to his bed to amend the terms of their agreement irrevocably. A shuddering breath escaped his lungs as he fought to bring his clamouring instincts under control. He couldn't indulge himself in this particular fantasy. It would be too easy to lose it all.

Declan put down his case and his laptop inside the door to his bedroom and turned sharply on one heel to stride back down the hallway and out the front door, closing it firmly behind him. He headed for his car then hesitated for a moment. No, on second thought, driving wasn't a good idea in his current state of mind. He removed his cell phone from his breast pocket and punched in a few numbers.

"Mason, I need a drink, probably more than one. Grab Connor and meet me at Joe's Bar, in half an hour."

Without waiting for a reply, he flipped his phone shut and strode down the footpath. Yeah, at this pace he'd make it into Newmarket in no time, and would hopefully have worn off some of the repressed energy that roiled through him like an angry tiger. And if he hadn't, then he could always pick a fight with one of his brothers.

Gwen sat up with a splash. Was that the front door? She listened carefully, but heard nothing. The bath water was getting cold. Time to get out. She levered herself from the bath and wrapped herself in a clean fluffy towel before pulling the bathroom door open.

"Declan? Is that you?"

No reply. Strange. His case was poking out slightly into the hallway. Gwen slipped down the hall and into her office where she could get a look at the driveway. Yes, his car was definitely there. But where was he?

She dashed into her bedroom and closed the door, determined not to be caught undressed when she next saw him. She pulled on her nightgown and wrapped herself up in her robe, tying the sash firmly around her waist. After slipping her feet into the blue monster-feet slippers Libby had given her as a joke last birthday she felt appropriately unglamorous and invulnerable. Necessary armour with Declan Knight on the prowl.

By the time she'd drained the bathtub and hung up her dress properly she'd come to the conclusion that Declan was definitely not home. He must have popped in briefly while she was having her bath and then gone out again.

A large yawn took her by surprise and, deciding to forgo dinner, she settled on an early night.

Laughter, followed closely by an intense shushing noise, disturbed Gwen several hours later. A key fumbled in her front door and she was instantly awake.

"Thanksh, guys. I'll be fine from here."

Declan! A somewhat worse for wear Declan by the sound of him. A tiny smile played across Gwen's lips as she heard a male voice firmly telling him to let them assist him to his room. By the sounds of him, he wasn't in a much better state. She popped her head outside her bedroom door.

"What on earth have you been up to?" she asked.

Connor stood like a frustrated shepherd in her front entrance, a quizzical look of defeat on his face.

"It's not my fault. I tried to stop them." He put his hands up in surrender.

"You did?" The look of wonder on Declan's face was a picture in itself. Gwen struggled to hide her smile as the man she assumed from his familiarly dark good looks was Mason, Declan's older brother, with his back to the wall, slid down to sit on the floor.

"Hi, Gwen, gee, you're pretty." Mason smiled lop-sidedly.

"Hello, yourself," she replied. Good grief. How was she going to oust three Knights from her house? One was bad enough.

"Don't worry about Mason, I'll see him home soon." Connor put an arm around Declan's shoulders. "Let me get this one settled and we'll be on our way."

"I'll help you." Gwen moved to Declan's other side

and looped her arm around his waist. "Good grief!" she exclaimed as she breathed the fumes that emanated from him. "Did he drink a distillery dry?"

"Something like that." Connor's ironic response indicated his disapproval.

Together they levered Declan through his bedroom door and sat him on the edge of the bed. While Connor supported him, Gwen pulled the covers away from one side of the bed. After swiftly divesting his brother of shoes, jacket, shirt and trousers Connor rolled him face-down across the bed and tossed the covers over him.

"There, that should see him through the night. Kinda cute when he's asleep, huh?"

She wouldn't have credited it unless she'd seen it with her own eyes, but, yes, Declan was already sound asleep. But cute certainly wasn't the first word that came to mind.

"You look like you've had some experience with this," Gwen commented.

"Yeah, well, we're all pretty good at it. Had a bit of practice with the old man after Mum died."

Gwen walked with him to where Mason still sat, leaning at an odd angle and humming quietly to himself. Connor gave his foot a nudge.

"C'mon, Mase. Time to get up and get you home, too." He offered his brother a hand and pulled him to his feet. "A Bullshot should fix Dec in the morning."

"Bullshot?" It sounded painful.

"Kind of like a Bloody Mary, but with tinned beef consommé as well. Works a treat."

"I'll take your word for it." Gwen pulled a face. It sounded dreadful. She watched as Connor controlled a weaving Mason back to the taxi waiting at the kerbside before shutting and locking the front door.

A worried frown creased her forehead. Would Declan be okay? What if he couldn't breathe properly lying on his stomach like that? Gwen sighed. She had to check on him or she'd worry all night.

Light from the hallway spilled across him. She needn't have been concerned—he'd rolled over onto his side. He'd pushed the sheets down, revealing the contoured muscles of his chest and arms. Gwen tiptoed into the room and stood at the side of the bed, listening for measured breathing. She couldn't hear a thing. She leaned closer, her face almost right next to his.

A brawny arm moved with unerring accuracy and speed to hook her around her waist and pull her onto the bed to spoon up against the length of his body. Gwen tried to pull free but his arm was an unyielding band across her. She wriggled slightly, and discovered in the same instant that had been a bad idea. A very bad idea.

His arm slipped to her midriff and pulled her firmly against him. One hand slid beneath her dressing gown and lazily cupped her breast. Through her robe and his bedclothes she could feel the heat that poured from his body to scorch a line down her back.

She tried to twist her head. Was he awake? No, the slow deep breathing that emanated from him indicated otherwise. It looked like she was stuck here for the night. Or at least until he loosened his grip. Gwen tried to ignore the charged pull of pleasure that his touch at her breast aroused. She had to try and get him to let go.

"Declan?" she whispered. No response but the warm rush of whiskey-laden breath against the back of her neck. "Declan?" she tried a little more loudly.

It was working, he was moving his hand. But not, unfortunately, away from the warm globe of her tingling flesh. His thumb had slipped up to stroke the sensitive bud of her nipple, the slow sweep creating a spiralling tension within her. A gasp caught on her lips as the drugging sweet sensation rippled through her body.

It had been too long since she'd felt like this. Too long and yet she'd promised herself that never again would be far too soon. But try telling that to the insistent beat of desire that thrummed through her veins, turning her insides molten with need. Need for him.

The past eight years fell away as if they'd never happened. In a single breath Gwen was transported back to when she'd gone to Declan's apartment in the city, concerned by how withdrawn he'd been since the accident. Worried that he might do something stupid, something to hurt himself. She'd been driven there by guilt. Renata had died because of her. She should have stopped her adventurous friend—had foolishly thought that Renata would listen to her as the voice of reason when she suggested they go back. But she'd been wrong. Totally, fatally wrong. And then, when Renata had needed her most, needed her strength to anchor them both to that pathetically tiny ledge, she'd failed her again.

The stark lines of grief on Declan's face when he'd answered the door had provided all the impetus she'd needed to attempt to console him. She'd opened her arms and he'd slid straight into them as if they belonged together. Even then she'd known it was wrong. That they were playing with fire. Tempting fate. But they'd each needed to forget, if only for a few hours, the horrific loss they'd suffered.

When their lips had met, hunger had flared with a voraciousness she'd never experienced before. But it had been the saltiness of the tears that tracked his cheeks that had been her undoing. At that point in time she'd have done anything—anything at all—to soothe his pain.

They hadn't even made it to the bedroom that first time. Instead, he'd pressed her against the wall, ripping her panties away and pushing up her skirt until he'd had access to her inner core. And she'd let him—welcomed him. She'd wrapped her legs around his hips and whispered gentle words of encouragement until they'd both reached a swift, almost vicious, climax. They'd stayed there, locked in each other's embrace, hard up against the wall, shaking with the after-effects of their joining.

It had created an addiction, that first coming together. A drug that needed to be purged from their systems as they'd loved through the night. Until the bleak honesty of morning had rent them apart. No one had ever touched her the way he had, or made love with such wild abandon. No one had ever given her such pleasure, nor such gut-wrenching desolation. She couldn't do it. She wouldn't survive. Not again.

"Declan! You must let me go." A tremor of uncertainty quivered in her voice.

"Just wanna hold you…so lonely." His words slurred and trailed away.

But something in her tone must have finally penetrated his mind as his arm loosened sufficiently for Gwen to free herself from his sleepy grasp and shoot to the edge of the bed. She forced herself upright and on shaking legs staggered to her bedroom where she closed her door, leaning back against the sturdy wood, desperate for something solid to anchor herself to.

Her breath dragged through lungs that were incapable of functioning. He was drunk, she rationalised. She had nothing to fear from Declan Knight. Her life, her plans, her security—everything was safe.

But what about her heart?

Eight

Declan's heart pounded as he stood before the ballroom bay window. He couldn't help but appreciate how appropriate it was that, given her love of historical homes, Gwen had chosen to marry in one of Auckland's finest. The atmosphere imparted its own air of permanence, longevity and survival against the odds. And this marriage would need all the help it could get to survive the requisite six months to satisfy his father.

Mason fidgeted at his right-hand side but settled at an almost inaudible admonition from Connor. Declan fought a grin, strange that the baby of the family was the one hell-bent on keeping them in line these days.

The smile faded as he remembered the last time Connor had done that and the condition he himself had been in. He should have crashed at Mason's place. It would have been better all round and might have prevented the big freeze-off he'd had from Gwen since the morning after when she'd slapped a Bullshot in front of him, the crack of the glass onto the kitchen table ricocheting through his tender skull, then headed out into the garden where she'd worked for the rest of the day. When he'd gingerly slipped off to work she'd been at the very back of the property, and hadn't even acknowledged his farewell, and by the time he'd arrived home from work she'd been asleep. Or at least been pretending to be.

He'd been determined to have it out with her last night. It was vital that today go smoothly and he needed her assurance that this frozen standoff wouldn't impact on the day and the image they had to project. He hadn't counted on her observing the tradition of not seeing the groom on the morning of the wedding. She'd gone to spend the night at Libby's straight after the wedding rehearsal. A rehearsal he'd been late to thanks to the ongoing investigation into Crenshaw's embezzlement. A forensic computer technician had tied up the computers for most of the day, but at least it was bringing them closer to discovering where Crenshaw had run off to.

Declan had discounted forcing a confrontation with Gwen at the rehearsal dinner. It was hardly the best place to discover what had driven his bride away. His bride. The notion rocked him to the soles of his shoes. After Renata he'd never imagined wanting to marry anyone, least of all Gwen. But circumstances had a way of dictating what happened in life, and this *was* only temporary.

Last night she'd avoided him as completely as she could while going through the motions of their ceremony. He'd had to hand it to the celebrant when Gwen had introduced him as her fiancé. The man had stuttered momentarily but had pulled it together and glossed over any questions about the sudden change in groom with faultless professionalism.

A sudden clench in his stomach brought the reality home. Within the next fifteen minutes, Gwen Jones would become Mrs Declan Knight.

"It's not too late to back out, Dec." Mason's whisper earned him a powerful nudge from both Declan and Connor. "Hey, don't pick on me—I was simply stating a fact."

"Can it," Connor said quietly. "She's here."

The bass drum pounding in Declan's chest morphed into the full percussion section of the New Zealand Symphony Orchestra as he turned and saw a vision hesitating at the door. Libby and another young woman he'd met for the first time last night smoothed Gwen's gown, front and back, before taking up their positions in front of her.

The pianist settled at the baby grand struck the first notes of a popular Shania Twain melody, and Gwen began her slow walk towards him. Towards the beginning of their marriage.

A bittersweet shaft of pain struck him as he remembered his first bride. A bride who'd never quite made it to the altar. They'd rescheduled their wedding several times, each happy to coast along in the effervescent thrill of being in love with life and each other. So why hadn't they stuck with any of their wedding dates? Why had they deferred the confirmation of their promise to one another so many times?

Declan watched Gwen as she drew nearer.

All these years he'd pushed aside the thought of her, of who she was, *of what they'd done*—telling himself it was because of the pain of the reminder of Renata. Of that fact that if it hadn't been for her Renata wouldn't have been scaling that mountainside, wouldn't have made a bad judgement. Wouldn't have slipped and nearly pulled Gwen down the mountainside with her, and wouldn't have sacrificed her life to save her friend.

Her friend who now stood beside him as his bride.

Outwardly Gwen appeared pale and serene, although the slight tremor in the purple and white flowers she held gave mute evidence to her shaking hands. She was beautiful.

Sudden, shocking truth flooded his mind. Despite everything, he still wanted her as much now as he had that awful night when she'd been the only glimmer of light and hope in the dark days after the accident. The shattering discovery rippled through him, prompting Mason to mutter quietly, "Are you okay?"

No, he wasn't okay, nor was he prepared to face the mind-numbing reality of the tidal wave of want that pulsed through his veins, filling his mind with the memory of how she felt in his arms. How she tasted on his lips. He had to pull it together—to get through the ceremony—before he frightened her away for good.

"Friends and family, we are gathered here…"

Declan zoned out the celebrant's introduction as he stood next to Gwen, concentrating instead on his bride. Her silver-blond hair was up in an elaborate display of loops and curls on top of her head, and a scattering of purple flowers were tucked here and there in its softness. More accustomed to seeing her with strands slipping and sliding from confinement to grace her slender neck, this style made her appear remote—untouchable and too controlled—although her chest rose and fell with rapid, shallow breaths, giving away her true state of mind.

The urge to reach out to her, to calm her fears, fought within him but he held his arms down, hands clasped lightly together at his back.

"Therefore if any person can show any just cause why these two cannot be married, let them speak now…"

Let them try, Declan challenged silently. This was too important to screw up now, no matter what his body urged him to do. He sensed Gwen stiffen as the celebrant paused for what seemed like an eternity. She lowered her eyelids, hiding the expression in them. Was she hoping someone would step up to the plate and stop the wedding? Maybe she hoped in her heart of hearts that Crenshaw would have realised the error of his ways and come storming in on his white charger. Declan fought back the ironic curl that played around his lips. Imagining Crenshaw on a horse was kind of stupid, in fact imagining the guy having an honourable bone in his body was plain ludicrous.

He drew in a deep breath and let his senses be calmed by Gwen's gentle floral fragrance. *Yeah, that was better.* Yet a bitter taste lingered in his mouth as a question nagged at the back of his mind, begging to be answered. Did she still love Crenshaw?

"Now I ask you both, do either of you know of any reason why you may not be lawfully wed?" the celebrant asked, a serious expression chasing the humour from his eyes, then to Gwen's barely audible "no," and Declan's distinctly more determined one, he gave a slow wink and a warm smile. "Let's get on with the proceedings then."

"Declan, will you have Gwen to be your wife? To live together as husband and wife, to love her, comfort her, honour and keep her, in sickness and in health, and forsaking all others keep only unto her, so long as you both live?"

Gwen's eyes flicked up to his, a sheen of moisture blurring their clarity. *Forsaking all others.* Others like Steve Crenshaw. Was that what she was thinking? "I will." He pitched his voice loud and clear through the room. Let no one be in doubt about this wedding.

The celebrant turned to Gwen and repeated the words. She stood, as still as marble, before replying softly, "I will."

"Declan, please take Gwen's hand," the celebrant instructed.

She passed her flowers to Libby and turned slightly to face him. His heart gave a twist. They were so close to success. He could almost smell it. A fine tremor ran through her as he curled her cold fingers around his. Echoing after the celebrant, Declan made his vow, all the while holding Gwen's tortured silver gaze with his.

"I, Declan, take you, Gwen, to be my wife. To have and to hold from this day on, for better for worse, for richer for poorer, in good times and in bad, in sickness and in health, to love and to cherish, till death parts us. I give you my promise."

One tear spilled from Gwen's eye and tracked slowly, like a liquid diamond, down her cheek. She gripped his hand so tightly now his fingers started to go numb. In a muted, trembling voice she made her vow to Declan, managing to not quite meet his eyes while she did so. Declan sensed, rather than saw, Mason slide the two wedding rings onto the open book in the celebrant's hands. A roaring sound in his ears drowned out the blessing of the rings. This was it. They were nearly there.

Reluctant to break the tenuous connection between

them, Declan gave Gwen's hand a gentle squeeze before reaching for her ring and sliding it onto her ring finger.

"I give you this ring as a symbol of our vows and with all that I am, and all that I have, I honour you." A deep pull from inside made his voice rasp over the last three words. A pull he ruthlessly ignored.

Gwen gave him a startled look and a hot flood of colour rushed up his neck. Her hand was steady now as she reached for his ring and Declan endured the damning sense of déjà vu as he held out his hand to receive it. Only one week ago she'd done this very thing. A spiralling coil of tension wound in his stomach as she pushed the ring over his knuckle and in a hushed tone spoke the words that finally and completely bound them together. *For the next six months, anyway.*

"I now pronounce you husband and wife. Congratulations, Mr and Mrs Knight!" The celebrant beamed to the assembled guests and led them in a burst of applause, then leaned in toward Declan. "You can kiss your bride now."

At last. They'd made it.

Declan stepped up closer to Gwen and with infinite care slid one hand around the back of her neck. She tilted her face towards his, her eyes massive in her ashen face. His thumb rested on her pulse and he couldn't be certain if the wild beat he felt came from her, or from him. Slowly he brought his lips closer to hers and he heard her sharply indrawn breath as he stroked his thumb over her satin-soft skin. Her eyes flew to his, fear and need each in turn tumbling through them. He could wait no longer and took her lips in triumph.

He moulded his lips to hers, coaxing them to gently part and to allow him access to the sweet recess of her mouth. He couldn't get enough of the taste of her, of the texture of her tongue against his. They'd done it. They'd succeeded.

She was his.

Gwen gripped the pen in her hand with white-knuckled fingers, and dragged the ballpoint across the marriage certificate. *Married.* She hardly believed it. Her face ached with the effort of maintaining a smile for the photographer. If he asked her to look lovingly at Declan one more time she would give him a single lens reflex all right, straight into the nearest floral arrangement.

During the past four days she'd gone to hell and back, wondering if she could carry this off. She glanced up at the man who was now legally her husband. He was laughing at something one of his brother's had said. A fist clenched around her heart.

The feel and the taste of him were still imprinted on her lips. Gwen pressed her lips together to rid herself of the sensation that lingered. It didn't work. Declan's kiss, and her fiercely hidden reaction to it, were part of the show necessary to make this wedding look real. They were in it for what they could get—nothing more, nothing less. She had to remind herself of that.

She was grateful the reception was being held in a marquee here on the grounds of Highwic House. Being forced into Declan's close company in a bridal car right now was the last thing she needed.

Two hours later, Gwen decided the reception appeared to be going well. Most importantly, they'd carried it off as hardly anyone had passed comment about the speed with which her original wedding plans, and groom, had changed. In fact, everyone seemed to adore Declan. He'd been at her side constantly during the course of the evening, and had charmed everyone with his wit and personality. The ease with which he did so made Gwen distinctly uncomfortable. No one seemed to even care that Steve had dropped out of the picture so suddenly, or perhaps they were too embarrassed to bring it up?

Even Declan's rather dour-looking father hadn't been able to find a crack in their façade. Tony Knight hadn't struck Gwen as the patriarchal nightmare that Declan had portrayed, but then obviously the Knight men were very good at hiding their true thoughts. Strange, Gwen thought, she'd imagined that his dad would have been less accepting than he appeared and certainly less friendly, since, by marrying his eldest son, she'd effectively diminished his control of Cavaliere Developments. His initial stony stare had broken into warmth when he'd welcomed her into the family with a hug and said, "So this is what my boy has been up to? I hope the two of you are very happy."

The string trio in the corner struck up a gentle waltz. Declan appeared at her side and took her hand in his.

"Our dance, I believe." He led her onto the dance floor and drew her into his arms. "Relax, look as if you're enjoying this. It'll be over soon enough."

Gwen tried to do as he instructed but with one hand resting lightly on his shoulder and the other held in his she was more aware of him than she'd allowed herself to be all day.

The "tombstone"-style suit he wore with its long dark jacket and high neckline waistcoat emphasized his height and strength with a lethal rawness a more traditional dinner suit lacked. Combined with the collarless white Nehru shirt, fastened with an onyx stud at the neck, and his long dark hair tied tightly back, he looked invincible. She wondered if that's why he'd chosen them for himself and his brothers. They'd looked like a posse of hardened lawmen as they stood assembled in a line when she'd come into the ballroom. She wondered what they'd have done if she'd followed her screaming instincts and done a runner instead of sedately walking in her bridesmaids' footsteps to the front of the room.

For a big man Declan danced beautifully, and she moved with him in time to the music without sparing a thought to the mechanics of what they were doing. What his proximity was doing to her was another thing entirely. The spicy, musky fragrance he wore subtly threaded around her, drawing her into his aura in such a way that they could have been the only two people in the marquee. She was afraid to breathe him in too deeply, to let him too far past the barricades. She needed some space between them.

From the corner of her eye, Gwen saw Mason lead Libby onto the floor and then Connor, after pausing to briefly kiss his wife, Holly, do the same with Mae. She groaned inwardly—escape wouldn't happen any time soon by the looks of things, as all the traditional formalities were being observed. Everything about the wedding had been textbook perfect—on the surface at least. A tiny sigh escaped her lips.

"Had enough?" Declan whispered in her ear.

"Yes." *Oh, yes.*

"Let's slip away then." He took her hand and they worked their way through the growing crowd on the dance floor and toward the door.

"Oh no, you don't." Mason cut in on his brother.

"No sneaking her away until we've each done our duty, big brother."

"Mase—" Declan protested and moved to block his brother's intention.

"Its okay." Gwen put a placating hand on his sleeve. "As much as we'd like to escape, everyone would think it odd if we left so soon, anyway."

"Are you sure?" Declan's eyes narrowed.

"Of course. I'll be fine." Gwen allowed Mason to twirl her away from her new husband.

It was strange how three brothers could look so similar and yet feel so different. Gwen had to pull her thoughts together as she danced with Mason, then Connor, before Declan reclaimed her.

"Regrets?" Declan asked as they circled the dance floor.

"Do I have that luxury?" Gwen hedged.

Declan laughed, a forced sound out of sync with the celebrating people swirling around them. He looked over her head and scanned the room. "Dad seems satisfied, so far. He's planned a surprise for us tonight. He'd skin me if he knew I'd told you about it but I thought you'd prefer to be forewarned."

"Surprise?" Gwen's stomach plunged. Why did she get the distinct feeling she wasn't going to like this?

"Does the phrase 'honeymoon suite' ring any bells?"

"Oh, no."

"Yeah, when he found out we weren't planning to go away he was a bit surprised we hadn't at least organised a weekend honeymoon. So, being Dad, he organised one for us."

Gwen swallowed. "You couldn't change his mind?"

"Should I have tried? We need this to look like a normal marriage, for your sake as much as mine."

"Yes." A lump of lead settled in her chest at the reminder. "What about our things? Did he think of those, too?"

Gwen wondered whether she'd be forced to spend the rest of the weekend in her wedding gown. Her thoughts skidded to a sudden halt. Of course, under normal circumstances, clothing would be the last thing they'd be thinking of.

"Don't worry. I found out after you and Libby had left the rehearsal, so I asked Mae to come back to the house and pack some things to send over to the hotel for you." Declan looked around the room again. "I think we might be allowed to make it this time. Are you ready to leave?"

"Definitely." The vehement response drew a raised eyebrow from Declan, but Gwen ignored him, instead returning to the top table to collect her bouquet.

"More tradition?" he asked, surprise in his voice.

"Just keeping up appearances," Gwen replied acerbically.

"Look! They're leaving!" a shout came from the side of the marquee.

Gwen was surprised by a laugh bubbling over her lips as everyone jostled into position to catch the bouquet. She turned her back to the crowd and tossed the flowers in a graceful arc through the air.

A collective "ah" of disappointment brought her spinning around to face everyone. A wide grin split Declan's face as Mason stood juggling the bouquet, looking for all the world as if he wished the ground would simply open up and swallow him whole.

"Let's get going while the going's good," Declan said, as he grasped Gwen by the hand and together they slipped out the marquee. The white stretch limousine that had brought Gwen and her bridesmaids to Highwic waited patiently now to take them to their hotel. Joyful well-wishers spilled out behind, tossing a flurry of flower petals as Declan handed Gwen into the glowing interior of the car. She gave a final wave through the back window as the car swept away. Her life would never be the same again. Everything she had been, everything she was, had changed forever.

In the softly lit interior Declan observed the silent creature who was now his wife. A fierce and unexpected stab of pride and possession hit him fair and square.

"Would you like some champagne?" he asked.

"Yes. I think that would be a good idea." The strain in her voice encouraged him to agree and he dealt with the cage and cork of the wine, which had awaited them in the back of the limo, in quick order. She needed to relax, they both did, and maybe this would help.

"Aren't you curious about where we're going?"

"Would it make any difference?" She continued to stare out the window, breaking her concentration only to accept a frothing glass of champagne from him.

Their fingers collided and Declan was struck by the surge of electric awareness that jolted him. He liked the sensation. More than liked it if he wanted to be truthful. His wife was becoming addictive. The admission was an unexpected, and unwanted, complication.

"No." His voice was rough. He named the exclusive inner-city harbour-side hotel Tony Knight had booked for them, using every ounce of his considerable power in the marketplace to secure the accommodation at such short notice. "He's booked a suite so we'll have plenty of room."

Gwen remained nonresponsive. A trickle of annoyance ran down Declan's spine. She *was* getting something out of this, too—her home and the promise of a long-term job contract once the Sellers project confirmed—so why the continued cold shoulder? They'd done what they had to do so far. Surely she could relax now.

The ride downtown was swift in the late Saturday evening traffic, and in the fifteen-minute drive they'd barely had time to sip their wine. At the hotel a doorman came to open Gwen's door and help her alight.

"Good evening, Mrs Knight. Mr Knight."

Declan smiled and placed his arm around Gwen's slender waist, ignoring the way her body stiffened at his touch. At the front desk the concierge beamed widely and after observing the necessities for check-in saw them to their seventh-floor suite overlooking the harbour himself. After he'd extolled the virtues of the room he opened the champagne in the ice bucket, poured two glasses, then withdrew.

"Hmm, with all this champagne, maybe we should be celebrating?" Declan commented.

"Is this how you celebrate all your *business* deals? With French champagne?" Gwen responded, her mouth twisted in a wry smile.

"No, but this one is rather special, don't you think?" He wandered over to the floor-to-ceiling glass windows. "Magnificent harbour. Funny how we live and work here but rarely take the time to enjoy it."

"Most people don't make the time."

"We can make the time, now." Declan gestured to the expanse of the large suite. "What else do we have to do?"

What else indeed? Colour stained Gwen's cheeks. Did her mind follow the same track as his? Declan thrust his fists into his trouser pockets before he did something stupid like reach out and grab her. She'd already made it obvious downstairs that his touch was anathema to her. He needed to keep his inner Neanderthal under control.

"I have to get out of these clothes for one thing," she said bluntly, plucking at the skirt of her gown. Gwen spun on her heel and in a swish of satin and chiffon she stalked to the bedroom, closing the door firmly behind her. The distinct click of the lock drew a laugh from Declan, a laugh he quickly stifled. It was no laughing matter, although he had to admit he loved it when she got all snooty like that.

In fact he… Shock reverberated through him as he fought to push realisation back where it belonged but cold fingers continued to pluck at his heart, piece by piece peeling away the reinforced shell he'd so carefully erected after Renata died. Declan sank heavily into a leather sofa. His hand shook as he lifted the glass to his lips, spilling the golden liquid on the cuff of his jacket. He stared as the wine soaked into the dark fabric, then slowly replaced his glass on the coffee table.

He had done the impossible.

He had fallen in love with his wife.

Nine

Declan stared out the window as the last of the summer yachts motored back to their marina berths near the Harbour Bridge in the dusky late evening waters; the vision gave him no peace.

In love with Gwen? No. He had to be crazy. This was a business arrangement and *only* that. He would not—could not—be in love with her. Wasn't it bad enough he'd betrayed Renata's memory with her? This was supposed to be the safe option—one designed to get them both what they wanted with no messy complications. To be in love with Gwen would definitely be a complication. He clamped down hard on his crazy thoughts, shoving them back deep inside where they belonged. Where they couldn't be real. He was confusing love with lust, and lust for Gwen Jones was something he knew all too much about.

"Declan?"

He shot to his feet. He hadn't heard her unlock the door. She stood next to the couch, presenting her semi-bare back to him, the shoestring-thin straps of her dress drooping off her smooth shoulders.

"Can you help me with these buttons? I can't reach them all." Her tone left him in no doubt that she'd rather have called housekeeping for assistance.

"Sure." He willed the tremor in his hands to settle and reached for the row of tiny pearl buttons.

It was both agony and ecstasy touching her warm, bare back, painstakingly sliding each wee fastener through its tight satin loop. Again, her subtle floral fragrance teased his nostrils and infiltrated his senses with intoxicating purpose. It would be so easy to place his lips to the nape of her neck, to drink deeply of her essence and luxuriate in her scent. His hands itched to spread wide beneath the fabric of her gown and push it aside so he could sweep his hands around to the front and relish the softness of her luminous skin and to cup her breasts.

One by one another button was undone, another inch of her revealed. His breath disappeared, as if sucker punched, when he caught a glimpse of the pale, rose-pink silk torselette she wore beneath her dress. The kind of thing that had multitudinous hooks and eyes. *Oh, yeah.* Exquisite torture. And totally out of bounds.

"Thanks, I think I can manage from here." Gwen stepped out of his reach and gathered the gaping bodice to her chest with fisted hands. "I'll be quick in the bathroom in case you want to take a shower," she said over her shoulder as she walked back to the bedroom.

"Shower. Yeah. Thanks." His mouth was as dry as the

Sahara and his body broiled with a different kind of heat. Staying here was not an option. Not until he was at least so exhausted that he could fall asleep on the sofa bed in the sitting room and know that he wouldn't attempt to affirm his wedding vows in the bedroom he'd already mentally declared off limits.

"Hey, Gwen!" She halted in the doorway. "Toss my bag out here would you? I'm gonna hit the gym for a bit."

"Sure."

She brought his duffel bag through and put it on the sofa, holding the bodice of her dress carefully to her body the whole time. All it would take was a tiny tug in the right place and that sinfully sexy piece of lingerie would be exposed to his hungry eyes.

"Will you be long?" she asked as she went back to the bedroom.

As long as it took. "An hour or so maybe," he grunted, as he peeled off his coat and waistcoat and un-buttoned the neck of his shirt. Maybe a lifetime.

"I'll see you later then." She slipped through the door. She'd left it ajar this time. He didn't know what was worse. Knowing he couldn't simply walk in and see her, or knowing he could.

When he got back from his workout, and it would be a killer—he could tell that right now—he'd order up room service. He wasn't sure about Gwen, but for once he'd hardly been able to eat despite the range of tasty food at their reception, and he was ravenous now. Ravenous in more ways than one. Which was why he'd be denying both appetites until he could recover some control.

He cast a narrowed glance at the bedroom door. The temptation was almost overwhelming. With an exasper-ated sigh he peeled off the rest of his clothes and slid into a pair of shorts and a T-shirt. It was going to take one hell of a lot to take the edge off that particular hunger.

Gwen stepped out of her wedding gown and looped the straps over a coat hanger before hanging the dress in the wardrobe. She felt empty, deflated. This wasn't how her wedding day was supposed to have gone. Her fingers lingered over the beaded bodice work before she slid the door closed and turned her back on it.

A small case waited on the luggage rack next to the wardrobe. She unlocked it and lifted the lid. The garment at the top was wrapped in tissue and sealed with a label from one of Auckland's premier lingerie outlets, the same place Libby and Mae had insisted she purchase her wedding lingerie from. A small card nestled on top. Gwen tore open the envelope and read it, *"We couldn't resist, and hope he won't either!"* The card dropped from her fingers unheeded as Gwen pushed aside the tissue. What had her friends bought?

A tiny mew of dismay fell from her mouth at the vision of sheer rose-pink chiffon. With shaking fingers Gwen lifted the peignoir from the case. It matched her bridal underwear perfectly. There was no way in this lifetime she was going to wear it. She laid it to one side on the bedcovers and reached for the next item, a silky soft stretch lace teddy. What on earth had those two been thinking of? The teddy joined the peignoir on the bed-spread as Gwen checked the next layer—more lingerie. Gwen sighed and looked at the collection with growing irritation. Mae obviously didn't value her life very highly if she had packed only lingerie.

Lord, what she wouldn't give for a pair of jeans and a sweatshirt right now. She looked at the digital alarm clock at the bedside. It glowed with mute confirmation that morning was a very long way away and she still had the rest of the night with her new husband to endure.

Blindly Gwen snatched up the teddy, at least it would be comfortable to sleep in, and strode towards the bathroom. There had to be a hotel robe she could wear, and if that's what she was wearing when she left tomorrow, then so be it.

After dealing with enough hairpins to build a small bridge she tossed her hair loose from its confines. She laid the purple flowers, now looking somewhat tired, on the vanity unit. She'd planned to press them and keep them as a memento of her special day—at least when she'd *originally* planned the wedding. Well, the day had been special all right, but not the kind of special she'd planned on. Without another thought, she swept the spent blooms into the rubbish bin and turned on the shower.

Extricating herself from the torselette proved tricky but determination won out in the end. She kicked off her stockings and panties then stepped beneath the delicious pulsing spray of the shower. Gwen lathered up some soap and stroked it over her skin. Under normal circumstances she wouldn't have been alone right now. Although the image that sprang to mind was not of her and her originally planned bridegroom.

Instead, in her treacherous thoughts, a powerful tanned forearm lay across her stomach while she leaned back against a strong expanse of chest. Dark hair would be mingled with hers in the shower spray and plastered against her shoulders while long fingers gently soaped her body, slicked between the juncture of her thighs. Stroked and caressed.

The resounding clatter of soap as it hit the floor of the shower startled her out of her daydream.

"Gwen! Are you all right in there?" Declan's muffled voice penetrated the bathroom door. Oh, God, hadn't he left yet? Please say she'd locked the door. No. In the instant she hesitated to reply he was through the door, worry stark on his face. "I heard a crash, are you okay?"

The heat of embarrassment flowed through her from the tips of her apricot tinted toenails to the top of her head. She opened her mouth to answer but nothing came out, whatever she'd been about to say lost in the blaze of his stare. The flush that suffused her body altered subtly—like a wind shift over a sandy beach—becoming, instead, a bloom of desire. Desire for Declan. Desire for her *husband*.

Her nipples creased into tight buds, tingling with the need to be touched. A tingling that travelled, spread, and bathed her whole body. She watched, helpless, as his gaze locked onto her breasts. She could almost feel the heat reflected in his eyes, almost feel the caress of his lips against her skin.

"Get out!" she cried, her voice harsh, desperate.

Without a word or a backward glance, Declan left and closed the bathroom door silently behind him. Under the steady stream of warm water, Gwen began to shake. She slid down the wall of the shower and crouched in a heap at the base. This was all wrong. What would it take to purge him from her system? When would her body no longer cry out for his touch?

Declan set the treadmill to its most gruelling level—anything to drag his struggling hormones under iron control—a task easier thought of than achieved.

He didn't even need to close his eyes to see her. She was imbedded firmly in his brain. Her long slender arms, her high firm breasts tipped with nipples that had darkened and tightened under his stare, the delicious indentation of her belly button in her smooth, flat stomach and— He *had* to stop this! It was driving him crazy.

She was driving him crazy. He wanted her like he'd never wanted another woman. In the eyes of the law she was his. But he knew to the depths of his soul that it took more than paper to belong to Gwen and he wasn't prepared to plumb those depths. Not back when Renata died, and certainly not now. There was nothing for it but to pound out the miles on the treadmill then bench-press her out of his system.

Ninety minutes later his muscles were screaming for release, and that wasn't all. He still wanted her, dammit. Declan flicked an eye to the wall clock mounted above the door. With any luck she'd be asleep by now.

When he let himself back into the suite he was surprised to find her curled up on the couch wrapped in nothing but a thick white terry robe. Well, not quite nothing but the robe, a tiny hint of pink lace peeked temptingly where the robe crossed her breasts.

"Feel better?" Her voice sounded thick, as if she'd been crying. Yeah, no doubt she had. It certainly wasn't the wedding night she'd been expecting a week ago.

"I need a shower. Okay if I go through?"

"Sure, help yourself."

Even the sharp cold-needled spray of the shower did nothing to diminish the heat that pulsed through his body. He was just going to have to be a man and grit his teeth and bear it. Six months wasn't long. He took a disparaging look at himself in the bathroom mirror. Okay, so six months in this state would be a very long time. But he'd get through it. He'd gotten through worse.

"I ordered up some room service. I hope you don't mind." Gwen greeted him as he came back through to the sitting room, the jeans he'd pulled on barely disguising his state of constant semi-arousal.

"Sure, whatever. I didn't get much to eat at the reception. You?"

"No, I wasn't hungry then."

But was she hungry now? And for what? He'd lay odds her hunger didn't have a patch on his. A discreet tap at the door, followed by "room service" snapped him out of his thoughts. He stood, unsmiling, to one side as the waiter placed their desserts in the discreetly hidden refrigerator, laid the dining table in front of the window and lit the candle set in the centre of the table. Declan tipped the fellow, but rapidly wished he hadn't as on his way out the door the waiter dimmed the central lights to create an altogether too intimate atmosphere.

"I'll turn the lights back up." Declan raised his hand to the switch.

"No." Gwen sighed. "Leave it. It's okay. Besides, the table looks lovely. By the way, I owe you an apology. I'm…I'm sorry I snapped at you before, back in the bathroom. You kind of took me by surprise."

"Don't worry about it." And don't bring it up again, *please,* Declan begged silently, willing his body back under control as it leaped to eager life at the memory.

Gwen lifted the covers on the plates and leaned forward to inhale. "Mmm, this smells divine. I haven't had crayfish in ages. I hope you don't mind, I was a bit extravagant on the order."

"Hey, we need to make it worth Dad's while." Declan

cracked a smile at the irony, sure that being extravagant hadn't come easily to Gwen and wondering what had prompted it. Maybe she'd just given in to a guilty pleasure for once. Was that what he'd been eight years ago? A guilty pleasure? He slammed down hard on the thought. He couldn't afford to go down that road. Instead, he pulled out a chair and gestured for her to sit. "Come on, then. Let's eat."

He gallantly endeavoured to resist the urge to peek from above as the lapels of her robe gaped as she sat down. He flunked miserably. Man, but he was a fool for punishment. A hint of lace against soft, creamy skin sent his blood pressure skyrocketing. He swiftly rounded the table and slid into his chair. Food. What he needed was food. He did not need complications and Gwen had become one heck of a complication.

No, that wasn't quite fair. How he felt about her was now the complication. Their marriage had to last six months. He'd do well to remember that. If she knew what she did to him, no doubt she'd be out that door so fast the dust of his growing empire would still be hanging in the air like yesterday's dreams. He would not let that happen.

"This is delicious," Gwen said as she tasted the crayfish mornay.

Declan tried to ignore the way her tongue swept her lips as she enjoyed the shellfish. Tried, and failed. "Yeah, they sure know how to put room service together here."

"I couldn't resist ordering dessert, too."

"Well, if it's half as good as this it'll be worth waiting for. What have they sent us?"

"Champagne zabaglione."

"Zabaglione?"

"Yeah, egg, sugar, champagne. Delicious. I haven't had zabaglione since I was a girl." Gwen's voice was wistful, her expression distant.

"Really? How come?"

"The last time I had it was in Milan, before my mother sent me away. When I came to New Zealand my aunt wasn't into anything that frivolous. Even an ice cream from a street vendor was out of the question as far as she was concerned."

"You've been to Italy, then?"

"I was born there."

Born there? Declan racked his brain to remember if she'd ever given any indication of her heritage. "How come you came to New Zealand?"

She sighed and put her fork down on her plate. "Okay. I'll give you the potted history. Mum met my father there while on a modelling assignment. Against his family's wishes they married when she fell pregnant with me. Unfortunately, she neglected to tell him I wasn't his. A little before I turned six he found out and threw us both out. For a while Mum's boyfriends didn't mind me around but when I was nine she sent me here to live with Aunt Hope. She promised she'd come for me one day, but I guess it really doesn't suit her image to have an adult daughter."

"God, Gwen, I'm so sorry. That must have been helluva tough."

"I wrote to her when Aunt Hope died, but the letter was returned unopened. I suppose that made her position pretty clear, and by then I'd learned not to need her in my life anymore." Or anyone else for that matter. Gwen straightened her spine, unconsciously assuming the rigid posture she'd adopted as a child to prove that nothing and no one could hurt her again. But she'd been wrong. Painfully wrong.

From the man she'd always thought of as her father, to her mother, right through to Steve, she'd been let down by those she'd learned to love and to trust.

"I take it dessert is off the menu then?"

Gwen's laugh was brittle. "No, of course not. I'm sure it will taste wonderful."

They decided to eat their desserts while watching a cable movie. Gwen curled her feet up under her on the couch, Declan ensconced in the opposite corner. She was surprised to discover how much fun it was to watch the film with Declan. He had a quick wit and his amazing comebacks to some of the lines in the movie had her chuckling away. In fact, if she admitted it, she was actually enjoying herself. The pressure of the day had faded away, the need to be perceived to be the besotted happy couple gone. They could simply be themselves. So where did that leave them?

While this was a suite, so far Gwen had only seen one bed. Surely they weren't sleeping together. After that unfortunate encounter in the bathroom, there was no way she was sharing a bed with Declan. She even wondered if the two of them continuing to share a house together was a good idea. The alternative, however—not sharing it—would arouse suspicion and throw all their plans in jeopardy.

As the movie drew to an end, tension built within her. It was getting late. They'd need to go to bed soon. She tried to tell herself the sensation bubbling in her stomach was nerves, but it felt deliciously like something else.

The credits began to roll up the screen.

"Do you want to watch another movie?" Declan asked, picking up the movie guide from the coffee table.

"What is there?"

"Hmm, nothing all that current unless you want to watch an action flick."

"I think I might go to bed. You, too?"

Declan sent her a telling glance, and she wished her words back firmly in her mouth. She'd all but invited him into bed with her!

"I might take advantage of the bathroom first." He arched one eyebrow at her. "Are we going to flip for the bed or shall we share?"

Gwen's pulse accelerated. Crunch time. She eyed up the couch they were sitting on, she'd probably be comfortable enough out here.

Declan's chuckle startled her. "Hey, I'm just teasing," he laughed. "This folds out to be a sofa bed, I can kip out here easily enough."

"Are you sure?" Gwen looked at the length of him, thinking he'd be far more comfortable in the super-king-sized bed in the other room.

"Not a problem. I've slept in worse places. I'll just use the bathroom, then it's all yours, okay?"

Without waiting for her reply he went through to the bedroom. To distract herself Gwen wandered around the room, taking in the quietly restful décor. Suddenly she noticed a red light blinking on the desk telephone. They had a message? Who would have rung? Had their ruse of a marriage been sprung already? She lifted the receiver and dialled the message service.

"Mr and Mrs Knight, please accept the hotel's apologies, but it appears that one of your cases was left at the porter's station. Please contact reception when you're ready to receive it."

Clothes. Mae could live another day. Gwen gave a grim smile; of course her friend wouldn't have left her completely in the lurch.

"Was there a message?" Declan came through from the bathroom. He'd changed into the other bathrobe. Her mouth dried as he padded towards her on bare feet. His long legs closed the distance between them. Was he going to sleep naked? Every nerve went on full alert.

"There's another case for us downstairs. I'll get them to bring it up now," she said, averting her gaze before her expression could give away the sudden rush of desire that flooded her body.

"Yeah, good idea," he replied and sat back down on the couch and stared at the television, surfing through a few channels until he found a news site.

Gwen tried to ignore the way his robe fell away from his torso to expose the fine dark hair that arrowed down his lower belly. Her fingers curled into tight fists as she remembered trailing her fingertips through the soft scattering of hair, lower and lower until she'd traced the inner line of his leg and finally cupped the full aching hardness of his arousal. Her ears filled again with the groan of need that had ripped from his throat at her tender touch, her mind with the power that came from knowing she had wrought that reaction from him.

Gwen sluggishly dragged her thoughts back to the present. What was she supposed to be doing? Clothes. Yes, that was it. She dragged her eyes from his body and swiftly made the call that with any luck would bring her some relief from his unsettling presence before she surrendered to foolish need—just like she had eight years ago.

Ten

Gwen perched on the edge of the bed the next morning. She'd been up and dressed for what felt like ages, yet filled with reluctance to go out and face Declan, and the new day, as his wife. She'd heard his cell phone ring about an hour ago, and the rumble of his voice through the door as he took the call, so she knew he was awake. When the doorbell to the suite rang she decided she'd hidden in her room long enough.

At the sound of the bedroom door opening Declan turned from where he stood in the doorway, his body masking that of another man. He turned back and said a few words she couldn't make out before he shut the door and came back into the parlour.

"Good morning." His eyes didn't meet hers.

Curiosity piqued, Gwen asked, "Who was that?"

"Detective Saunders."

Gwen recognised the name immediately. He was the lead detective in the case to find their money—and Steve. "He came here? Today? How'd he know we were here?" Of course, Gwen realised, the phone call.

"He had information he felt we should know now. And he…" Declan paused and took a breath deep into his lungs. "He wanted me to I.D. Steve in a photo."

There was a strange tone to his voice. A tone that made the hairs on the back of Gwen's neck prickle and her blood run cold. "Was it Steve?"

"I believe so."

"You believe so? What do you mean *believe so?*"

"The picture wasn't particularly good quality. But they think they've found the money. It seems Crenshaw had opened an account in Switzerland. Interpol are working on the details now."

"And have they arrested him? Are they bringing him back?"

"Not exactly. Look, Gwen, there's no easy way to tell you this. Steve's dead."

"Dead?" All the air sucked from her lungs, and her legs threatened to buckle beneath her.

Declan reached out, taking her firmly by the upper arms and forcing her down into a chair. "C'mon, Gwen, don't lose it on me now. Take deep breaths, nice and easy."

She focussed on his voice, his strength, and breathed in and out until the sick sensation in her stomach settled with a flutter.

"How did he die?" Her voice wobbled as her throat constricted.

Declan took a deep breath. This was the pits. How the hell did he tell her? The picture taken of Crenshaw had been a crime scene photo and it hadn't been pretty. "Apparently he got caught up in a bar fight. It was quick."

"What will happen now? Will they bring the body back?"

A sickening sense of déjà vu tipped his stomach as he remembered a similar conversation. One where Gwen had clung to the rocky ledge that had saved her life when she and Renata had fallen—the ledge Renata had missed and dangled beneath until she'd eventually plunged beyond, her body finally coming to rest in a crevasse lower down. Gwen's refusal to leave the mountainside until he gave his promise that Renata's body would be recovered still rang in his ears. His heart twisted at the memory and his voice roughened. "He didn't have any family. They'll bury him there I imagine. Unless you want me to bring him home."

Gwen rose from the seat and with her arms wrapped about her torso as if holding in her pain, she paced back and forth before stopping in front of him. "You'd do that?"

Declan battled with the urge to shout "no." To tell her to leave the guy where he belonged, in an unmarked grave where his deceit could be buried along with him. "If you want me to, yes."

"And the money? Can they retrieve that?"

"By the sounds of things, yes."

"Then we didn't need to get married after all." Gwen's voice shook again, as if she was close to tears.

Declan clenched his jaw. Technically, they *could* both walk away from their marriage today. Over. Finished. "It's not as simple as that," he finally ground out. "Getting the money back could take months. Time we don't have."

"So we have to keep on with this—" she gestured

widely with one hand, clearly lost for a suitable explanation.

"Yeah. We do."

She bowed her head slightly and closed her eyes. What was going on in that pretty head of hers? Regret, he had no doubt, and probably a fair smattering of frustration. But what about grief? His blood boiled at the thought of her wasting a speck of emotion on Crenshaw.

Gwen drew in a sharp breath, her chin kicked up again and she turned to face him.

"Let Steve be buried by the authorities."

"Are you sure?"

"Yes."

"Okay, then. Let's go home. I'll get the concierge to call us a cab." Declan watched as Gwen walked back to the bedroom to gather her things. He called her just as she reached the doorway. "Gwen? Are you okay?"

She stopped and hesitated a moment before answering. "I have to be, don't I?"

Declan sat back on his heels to admire the finish on the blackened iron surround of the fireplace. He'd worked like a demon this past week—they both had— and this was the last job to complete the whole room.

They'd been lucky to find replacements for the cracked tiles that decorated the sides of the fireplace at a demolition yard on the other side of town. When she'd discovered them her face had lit with enthusiasm—the first genuine uncontrolled emotion she'd shown since the wedding and since the news of Steve Crenshaw's death. A rueful smile tugged at his lips. He'd take her back there every single day if it meant he'd see that response on her face again. She'd sprung to life, full of energy, full of excitement—a complete contrast to the automaton who'd worked doggedly at his side the past seven days.

Her attention to detail had been flawless and spoke volumes as to the standard of work he could expect from her on the Sellers project—if they got it. The result of the tender would be announced tomorrow and he didn't know what churned him up more. The hope they'd get the job and he'd get to work closely with Gwen on a daily basis, or the fear that they'd failed. He looked up as Gwen came into the sitting room, a tray with lunch in her hands.

"Hey, you've finished. The fireplace looks great."

Declan wiped his hands on a rag towel and took the mug she proffered. "Yeah, we're all done in here."

She put a plate of sandwiches on the table and perched on the edge of the sofa, her slender fingers clasped around her mug. Declan reached over to snag a sandwich and bit into it as he looked around the room. The walls glowed with a welcoming, gentle golden hue, and a faint hint of the scent of fresh paint still hung in the air. The tall sash window frames were sanded and sealed, and a heavy swag of drapes hung on iron rods from the top. They'd been a struggle to get up, but between the two of them, they'd managed. The deep skirting boards had been brought back to their warm natural wood, as had the feature point of the room, the mantelpiece. Yeah, they'd done okay.

"If I couldn't see it, I wouldn't have believed we could have achieved this much in a week." Gwen smiled, transforming the pinched, haunted look that lingered about her eyes to one of genuine pleasure.

"We make a good team. Do you want to light the

fire tonight to celebrate?" Declan sat back to admire his handiwork.

"Could we?" she burst eagerly, a teasing twinkle uncharacteristically lighting her grey eyes. "It's not really cold enough yet. Besides, it'll make it all dirty and spoil your hard work."

He snorted. "So I'll clean it again. What do you say? I saw plenty of dry chopped wood in the shed out back." It was great to see some life back in her face, however fleeting he knew it would be.

Gwen nodded. "I'd love to. I never imagined I'd be able to enjoy the fireplace so soon."

"Well, you didn't count on having a master renovator on the scene, now did you?" Ah, heck, now he'd gone and done it. Gone and put his foot firmly in his mouth with another stupid reminder of Crenshaw.

"No." She looked pensive for a moment before her habitual impenetrable shield slid over her face. He hated it when she hid like that. Then, to his surprise, she looked up and met him squarely, eye to eye. "I haven't thanked you for everything you've done. I…appreciate it. Everything."

The watery shimmer in her eyes spoke volumes. He put his mug down and wrapped his hands around hers. Despite the warmth from her coffee mug, her fingers were chilled. Kind of like she'd been most of the week.

"Hey. We have a deal, right?"

"Yes, we do." Gwen blinked away the moisture clouding her eyes and smiled back. "Are you on wood duty, or am I?"

"You are. I'm still busy."

"Busy eating!" Gwen laughed and his insides clenched in response. He wanted to hear that laughter more often and, more than that, it forced him to acknowledge he wanted to be the one who instigated it.

All week he'd been pushing back how he felt about her, distracting himself instead in the satisfaction derived from the work they'd completed together. Even the little things, like anticipating her pleasure when he found a tarnished brass doorplate, still attached to a borer-ridden door, at the demolition yard and knowing it was a perfect match for the broken one already attached to the sitting room door.

A perfect match. Would she ever see him any differently? Did he even want her to? He'd loved Renata for so long and still missed her with a physical pain, but day by day he was forced to recall her face and the sound of her voice, to rid his thoughts of images of Gwen. He'd avoided trying to understand why his thoughts had taken that crazy path on their wedding night when he'd confused lust with love. The lust was still very definitely there, though. Simmering beneath the surface like molten lava just waiting to push through the earth.

He stole a look at Gwen. She was too thin. The last couple of weeks had taken their toll and the week to come was set to be equally as tough. Declan didn't want to dwell on what would happen if he didn't win the tender or where it would leave this empty shell of a marriage. Logic told him to give it up. To remember their contract and to stick to it. Remember the reason why they were even together at all. Yeah. He remembered all right, and it left a bitter aftertaste in his mouth. A taste he wanted to be rid of.

He put his mug and plate back on the tray. "Why don't we order dinner in tonight and open a bottle of wine to christen the room?"

"I'd like that." Gwen put her own unfinished lunch on the tray next to his empty plate and gathered up the tray. "I'll go and grab some wood for the box, while you finish up."

Dinner finished, a contented sigh slid past her lips as firelight gleamed through the rich garnet-coloured Shiraz in her wineglass. It seemed fitting that Declan share this moment. Her sitting room looked as she'd always imagined it would with the addition of a multistemmed wrought-iron candelabra, a wedding present from Connor and Holly, taking pride of place on the mantelpiece, the votive candles flickering golden light across the walls while floating candles in a red and gold patterned glass dish on the coffee table cast a subtle gleam over the rest of the room.

"Happy?" Declan's deep voice interrupted her train of thought.

Was she? Gwen paused to reflect for a moment and realised with surprise that for the first time in forever she truly felt happy. "Yes," she answered, feeling the deep-seated contentment expand through her chest.

"A toast then?"

"Sure, what shall we toast?"

"To the continued success of Mr and Mrs Knight." His tone was light, teasing, but there was a glimmer of something more in his eyes. A glimmer she neither wanted to acknowledge nor answer.

Gwen hesitated for a moment. She couldn't, and didn't want to, get used to the moniker—Mrs Knight. All too soon she'd be plain old Gwen Jones once more. Declan's glass was still upraised to meet hers, the light in his eyes firing into a dark challenge.

"To us," she amended and clinked her glass against his before taking a sip of her wine.

Despite the fact the dust covers were finally, permanently, off the furniture, Gwen and Declan sat on the thick carpet rug in front of the fireplace. Heat from the fire caressed her skin while a warm glow from the wine grew inside her. It was probably extravagant to have lit the fire so early in the season, with summer still clinging to each day, but Gwen didn't care.

This was homage to the realisation of part of her dream. Her home. And she'd never have achieved it without the man at her side. How he'd found the patience to deal with her all week was beyond her. Steve would never have tolerated her melancholy. Never have striven, daily, to surprise her out of her mood.

No. Declan was different. And not only in appearance. There was a sensitivity, a softness, about him. A need to protect and provide that he usually kept well hidden from view. She was beginning to understand why. He'd talked a little about his mother this week as they'd worked together. How young he'd been when she'd died. How he'd assumed responsibility for his brothers while their father had buried his grief in work and, occasionally, in drink. That responsibility had carved him into the man he was today. Her husband.

They'd worked as a team, anticipating one another's actions. Anticipating one another's needs. As hard as she'd fought it, she was losing the battle to keep him at arm's length.

He wore his hair loose tonight. It lay like a black river down his back. Firelight bronzed his skin. Instinctively Gwen used her free hand to stroke the length of his hair, its softness making her palm tingle. She hadn't realised how much she'd needed to touch him, until now. Declan turned his head, his lips finding the point at her wrist where her pulse beat with a steady throb.

"Yeah. To us," he echoed.

He reached up and took her glass from her hand and set it on the table behind them. Her heart skipped a sudden fast beat, then settled. He was going to kiss her. She knew it and, while common sense shrieked at her to pull away, she didn't want to stop him. Not now. Not ever.

Bit by tiny bit, he'd worked his way under her skin and permeated her world. A gentle touch here, a smile there, and all the time deep consideration for her. At one stage she wanted to scream because he treated her so gently, but she'd slowly realised he was giving her time. Time to let go of the past—let go of Steve.

But was it time to look forward to the future? The future raised so many other questions. They would part at the end of six months. She'd be alone, again. Couldn't she just have the here and now?

They'd been married a week, and she felt more comfortable with him than she had with any other person her whole life. With a single glance he heated her blood. The accidental brush of his fingers set her pulse racing and her nerves to tighten and tingle. When she'd agreed to marry Steve she'd chosen not to experience the feelings Declan Knight built within her. She'd been a fool to think such an option would have satisfied her. That to hide from emotion, from the heat of passion, was better than to embrace the vulnerability that answering her body's clamour would surely bring her.

She'd given in to Declan once. The shattering fallout of that union had been enough to send her scuttling back to where only she could heal her wounds and, with that healing, vow to never allow her heart to be so exposed again. She didn't know if she could rip open the healed skin of that wound again. The finite period of this marriage was set. The boundaries were drawn. But maybe now it was time to overstep them. To relinquish past dreams, past failures. Time to believe in herself. And who better to do that with, but Declan.

As his lips closed over hers she let her eyes slide shut. He took her lower lip gently with his teeth and his tongue slid, hot and wet against the tender skin. He tasted of wine, of him, of forbidden dreams.

She let her tongue sweep against his and drew deep satisfaction from the sigh that filtered from him. She had the power to do that. To draw a response from deep within and past the barriers she recognised she wore herself. The realisation she affected him so strongly gave her a surge of power. *She* could control this. *She* could let this lead them wherever they wanted.

Gwen knew in her heart that if she asked him to stop now, he would withdraw. This was up to her entirely. She opened her mouth a little wider, drew in a little closer to him. Her hand reached up and tangled in his hair, and she kissed him as she'd kissed no other man.

He let her lead the way, set the pace. The thrill that gave her sent an electric dart of pleasure through her body. Without letting her lips break contact she rose and straddled his hips, relishing the heat that emanated from his body in front of her while through the thin fabric of her T-shirt the fire warmed her back.

Still he didn't touch her directly. If he hadn't relinquished that sigh of pleasure she would have pulled back. Removed herself from a situation that might only serve to reiterate her failures.

She was hot. Too hot. She drew back from him long enough to slip her T-shirt up over her torso and off. His eyes glittered like black diamonds in the flickering firelight as she bent towards him and pushed him gently backwards onto the floor. She pressed her lips to the strong column of his neck and let her tongue trail a fine path to the base of his throat. To the spot she'd dreamed of tasting again. Her hands stroked his chest through his shirt and through the fabric she could feel his nipples harden. Satisfaction at his reaction pulsed through her. She could conquer anything, anyone. Even him.

The need to touch him, flesh on flesh, overwhelmed conscious thought. Buttons slid excruciatingly slowly from their holes until finally she eased the fabric away from his body and could indulge in the sheer pleasure of stroking the pads of her fingers across his skin.

Tiny goose bumps rose on his flesh at her tender touch and she smiled at his reaction. She wet one finger in her mouth, drawing it slowly from between her lips, watching him watching her. The expression on his face did crazy things to her insides, making her clench and release muscles throughout her body in a vain attempt to cap the sensations that threatened to take her over.

With gentle pressure she circled one taut brown nipple with her dampened finger, then repeated the exercise with its twin. She leaned forward, letting her hair brush against him, then blew a cool stream of breath across the moistened discs. To her delight they tightened further, and she felt an answering constriction in her own as they pressed against the fine lace of her bra. The pleasure pain of the friction of her nipples against the fabric drew a small shudder through her body. She reached behind her and unclasped the hooks that fettered her, letting the straps drop down her shoulders and her bra fall forward, loosing her aching breasts to Declan's glazed, half-lidded stare.

"You're so beautiful." His voice was raspy, as though talking was an effort.

"Shh," Gwen commanded as she bent towards his lips once more.

She traced their outline with the tip of her tongue, her breasts barely touching his chest until she could bear it no longer. She leaned against him, harder, until her soft flesh pressed against his. Instead of relieving the throb it only intensified. A small sharp cry fell from her mouth as need pounded through her. She reached down and un-snapped the button fly of her jeans, rolling away from Declan only long enough to shimmy free of the restriction of the denim.

Everything in Declan urged him to take control. She was killing him with her gentle assault on his body. But for the life of him he couldn't think of a better way to go.

The tiny triangle of lime-green bikini panties glowed like a fresh spring leaf against the incandescence of her skin. As enticing as they were, they had to go. His hands twitched as if of their own volition they could drag them slowly from her body. But this was her game, he reminded himself. A game to be played by her rules. He sure as hell didn't want to throw her off her stride.

A pang of need shot to his groin and set up a pulse as primal as a jungle beat radiating through him as she slid the scrap of lingerie down those glorious long legs of hers. The fire cast a halo around her. She looked sinfully beautiful—a fallen angel. Her long, fine hair slid across his stomach, setting up a chain reaction of goose bumps flowing over his skin, as she bent to loosen the button fly on his trousers. Declan stifled another groan. If she didn't get these pants undone soon she'd have to cut them off him. Then, wonderfully, oh, yeah, he was free. His swollen flesh sprang from the torture of his clothing. He was ready for her. So ready he thought he would lose control.

He lifted his hips as Gwen pulled his trousers and boxers down and finally off. Gracefully, she hooked one leg over him again, her knees clenched at his sides. Rising slightly she guided him to the hot entrance to her body and as their eyes locked in silent duel he knew she gave him far more than entry to her body. She gave him her trust.

Her eyes had darkened to charcoal and the hot flush of desire streaked her cheeks and across her chest. She stared at him, a tiny smile curving her sensuous full lips, as she slowly lowered her body over him, accepting him within her. A long, slow shudder shimmered through her as she sank down the full length of him. He could feel her, hot and wet, stretching to adjust to his size. God, she felt so right he almost lost it right there.

With his fists clenched into balls at his hips and all his muscles screaming in protest, it took every ounce of his control not to grasp her by the hips and take them both hurtling over the edge of reason. But if he'd learned anything from this past week it had been how vital it was to Gwen to have control.

The way Crenshaw had used her and the way he, Declan, had taken over her life since, had stripped her of her strength—something he knew had happened more than once in her lifetime. He could give that back to her. Here. Now.

Gwen trailed her fingertips over his chest, down over his ribs, across his waist and then to the spot where their bodies joined. Never losing eye contact he watched as she touched herself there, felt rather than heard the moan that slid from her throat. He couldn't help it, his hips thrust upwards, once, twice. Her hands dropped to his. She uncurled his fingers and drew them up to cup the burning flesh of her rose-tipped breasts. He gently massaged the full smooth globes as she leaned against his hands, her slight frame pressing against him as she allowed her body to rock in ancient rhythm with his.

Clawing demand for release swelled within him, but he refused to submit to it. Not until he'd seen Gwen reach her peak. She moaned and tilted her pelvis slightly, taking him even deeper into her body. The sensations that racked him clamoured to let go, but not even they were as exquisite as the expression on Gwen's face. Their joining felt so right. So complete. In this minute he finally understood he loved her more than he'd ever loved any woman. He wanted her in his life, like this, forever.

He now bore her full weight against his arms as she moved with increasing strokes against him until finally he felt her body clench and quiver. A deep-seated cry ripped from her throat as tiny tremors rippled through her body and dragged him over the brink—into blissful oblivion.

Satiated, he wrapped his arms around her and drew her trembling body against the length of his. Perspiration sheened their skin, firelight gilded them with gold. Her breathing slowed and steadied into a less frantic rhythm. Finally, she was where he'd ached to have her for longer than he'd wanted to admit. Secure, in his arms.

Much later, as the night air cooled, a sudden crack of constricting wood disturbed Declan's slumber. With sleep-drugged delight he trailed his hand over Gwen's hip and followed the line of her spine. She moved against him sinuously, stirring his body to full and eager wakefulness.

He rolled slightly so Gwen's body was cradled beneath his. With tender care he lowered his lips to the shell-pink nipple of one breast, twirling his tongue around the sensitive flesh, watching as it immediately tightened and budded against his ministrations. He drew the small, hard point into his mouth, suckling gently before releasing it with another swirl of his tongue. Only half-awake, Gwen pressed her body towards him, pressed her hips against his and moaned sweetly.

"Not yet, my love." The barely audible words whispered past his lips as he moved to take her other nipple in his mouth, laving the same care and attention as he had to its glistening twin.

He wanted to see her eyes glazed with need. Need for him. But not yet. Gently he nuzzled her neck, sipping at the intoxicating texture of her skin, before pulling away slightly to position himself between her open thighs. His tip nestled against the heat of her body and he pressed forward, ever so slowly, until he filled her. Bearing all his weight on his arms so that the only point where they touched was the one where they were joined, Declan rose above her.

A slight chill in the night air passed between their bodies, her skin tightened in response and she sighed, her breath a gentle whisper past his ear.

"Steve?"

Steve! Declan wrenched himself free of her body. *Steve?* She'd been pretending he was Steve Crenshaw all along? Was that why she'd taken him so boldly this evening, why she hadn't murmured so much as a single protest when he'd started to wake her with his lovemaking? Had she clung to the dream that he was another man?

Reality sliced through him with painful precision. He'd used her once before, to forget—now she'd done just the same to him. Somehow, knowing that didn't make it any better.

"I'm not Steve." The words broke aloud from his lips before he could stop them, before he could give in to the urge to wipe all memory of the other man from her mind, from her body.

Gwen fought the confusion that tumbled through her mind as the horror of the dream she'd been locked into dissipated. The nightmare where she'd relived her wedding night and, instead of retiring to a lonely bed, Declan had brought her body to life, craving the dizzying heights of passion. But when she'd reached for him, it had been Steve instead whose body hovered over hers.

The echo of Declan's voice hung in the air. A sickening sense of wrong-doing dragged her awake.

"I'm no man's substitute." Declan's voice rasped across her ears like bare skin over barbed wire. The accusation in his eyes was illuminated by the dying embers of the fire, which glowed sullenly in the grate.

Speech failed her and she watched helplessly as Declan drew himself to his feet and left the room. *No!* she cried silently, feeling the loss of his body, his presence, as keenly as if she'd lost a limb. She wanted to scream aloud, but she was terrified that if she did, once she started she'd never be able to stop.

Eleven

Gwen sat at the table, hunched over a cooling cup of coffee when Declan came into the kitchen the next morning.

After he'd left her last night she'd dragged herself to her bedroom, wrapped up in her dressing gown and curled, shivering, on her bed until pale streaks of pink striated the sky. In the cold reality of dawn she had wandered into the kitchen and had sat there ever since, trying desperately to find an explanation for what she'd done and said. But there was none. She'd acted foolishly, daring to reach for what she wanted, daring to take it, then look what had happened—she'd lost yet again.

Declan stopped beside her. Dressed as he was in a starkly tailored suit and a brilliant white shirt adorned by his signature jewel-bright tie, she couldn't identify with this corporate Declan. Not after the past week when they'd worked together, laughed together. Not after last night, when they'd loved together.

She stole a glance at him. His face held no clue as to what he was thinking.

She sighed. "About last night, Declan—"

"It didn't happen. Having sex was a mistake, Gwen. We both know it—it just clouds everything. We should've learned from past mistakes." He held himself rigidly, as if each word had to be scoured from deep within him.

It didn't happen? How could he say that? It had been the most defining thing she had ever done in her life— and it *had* been beautiful, even if the aftermath had left her emotionally burned. It didn't deserve to be diminished. And neither did she.

Gwen shot to her feet. "Had sex? Declan, we made love. And it was not *your fault*. It was something we did together because we wanted to. Because we wanted each other." Her clipped words seemed to have no effect.

"Whatever." He shrugged off her defence of their passion. "But like last time, we shouldn't have done it. Have you considered that we did so without protection?" He drew his dark eyebrows together in a slant. "This marriage is for six months, Gwen. Six months only. We can't afford consequences."

A shard of ice penetrated her heart. Consequences? No, they certainly couldn't afford that. She slowly counted to ten and focussed on her breathing—in, out— difficult as hell when her chest felt as though she were pinned down by an elephant.

She summoned the dregs of her courage and looked him straight in the eye. "Thank you for the reminder. You'd think I'd have learned after *last time*. And you don't have to concern yourself with consequences. I've been on the Pill since Steve and I met."

At the mention of Steve's name, Declan became even more rigid, if that were possible.

"Good," he said abruptly. "We're clear on that, then." He turned to leave but hesitated in the doorway. "And, Gwen, it will never happen again, I promise you. We will stick to the terms of our agreement."

She listened as his footsteps retreated down the hallway. It wasn't until his car roared to life and sped away with a squeal of tyres that she sank down into her seat again, and the trembling began to rock her body in violent waves. He'd made his feelings abundantly clear. And that was what she'd wanted all along, wasn't it? As her heart screamed to the contrary, Gwen forced herself to concentrate on facts. They'd had a deal. All they'd had to do was stick with it. How hard could it have been?

Declan shifted through the gears as quickly as he could to increase the distance between himself and Gwen. He'd been nuts to let her under his guard and allow the parameters of their paper marriage to shift. Totally certifiable. Just five months and three weeks and he was out of there for good, and after last night he couldn't wait to put this episode of his life behind him.

The visual memory of Gwen's golden-lit body poised over his, the glitter in her eyes, the scent of her skin, the exquisite feel of her as she'd lowered herself onto him flooded his mind. The sensation so vivid his whole body jerked, and he fought to drive a straight line. His body coursed with need so raw it shredded at his insides like a starved wild creature.

And all along she'd been imagining he was someone

else. Remember that, he counselled himself. His cell phone started to vibrate in his breast pocket, and he eased off the accelerator, pulling over to the side of the road.

"Yeah," he growled as he flipped open the phone.

"Mr Knight. Congratulations. I know you're anxious for the news so I thought I'd let you know straight away—your tender has been accepted." The rest of the excited Realtor's words filtered out as a rush of relief flooded through him. They'd done it. It was exactly what he'd wanted—what he'd worked so hard for and fought past even Steve Crenshaw's interference to win. So why did he feel as if he'd lost everything?

Ever since what she now privately referred to as 'the morning after,' she and Declan had observed a polite, if cool, living arrangement. Tonight would be the ultimate test as they were expected to dine with the board of directors and their wives. She and Declan would be the youngest couple there, and the most watched. It terrified her that Tony Knight would be able to see right through them, to see past the plastered up cracks in their façade and call them barefaced frauds and liars.

At the sharp knock on her bedroom door she let her hand drop and took a deep, steadying breath.

"I'll be there in a minute." In front of the mirror Gwen nervously smoothed her hair then coated her lips one more time with a glistening lip-gloss and stood back to appraise her reflection. Yes, that would have to do. If she failed to project the right image tonight it wasn't for lack of trying.

"The booking's at eight. We need to get going." Declan's growl echoed through her closed bedroom door.

Gwen's heart gave a painful twist. A month ago, in that heady week after their wedding he'd have knocked and then come in, not perpetuated this cold distance they'd maintained ever since that night. How many ways could he punish her for what she'd done, she wondered as she hesitated with her hand on the doorknob. How many ways could she punish herself?

"I'll wait for you in the car."

Gwen opened the door. "It's okay. I'm ready now."

For an infinitesimal moment she saw a flare of reaction in his eyes, a tightening of his jaw, before any animation was swamped by cool composure. But it was enough to have caught that glimmer, to know her efforts weren't wasted. She'd gone all out for this dinner. She was armoured to the hilt in a designer dress she'd borrowed from Libby. The fabric changed colour as she shifted, at first an intense periwinkle-blue, then a silver-grey, while the clinging fit of the sleeves and low-cut neckline emphasised her shoulders and, as of recently, more prominent collarbones. Her friend had laughingly said she looked like a blue flame, joking she'd be cool to appearance yet hot to touch. Libby's comment couldn't have been further from the truth—she wouldn't be igniting any passion in her husband tonight.

Declan gave her another hard look, then turned to hold the front door open, waving her through before him. Even though he barely spared her two words strung together these days, he remained faultlessly courteous. Sometimes it made Gwen just want to scream.

At the restaurant Declan handed the car keys to the parking valet and crossed towards her as she waited at the front door. He put a hand against the small of her back, the sensation of sudden heat making her flinch slightly.

"You're going to have to do better than that. They're expecting to see a happy couple."

"Well, that's going to be interesting then, isn't it?" The sharp response slid from her lips before she could stop herself.

"Gwen..." Declan started, his voice filled with warning.

"Don't worry, I know the rules. They won't suspect a thing." Gwen crossed her fingers that would be true.

As conversation buzzed around the table Gwen couldn't help missing the camaraderie they'd built up before this new cold war, the closeness that would have allowed them to exchange a look or a smile over the pomposity at the dinner table. Instead he'd studiously avoided making eye contact. Oh sure, to all intents and purposes they still managed to look like a happily newlywed couple. With his arm draped across the back of her chair, his fingers stroking the bare line of her shoulder to her neck and back again, anyone would have been forgiven for thinking that he couldn't keep his hands off her. If only his touch hadn't set up such a current of awareness coursing through her veins.

"So, Gwen," Tony Knight leaned across the table, "tell me how my boy's behaving. He's treating you right, yes?"

Gwen felt Declan's fingers still in their track across her skin and tighten on her shoulder. A lick of anger flamed inside. Didn't he think she could cope with such a question? "He's doing all the right things," she fenced with a tight smile.

Declan's father's face went still for a moment, then he leaned back in his chair and let rip with a loud guffaw. When he could contain himself again he lifted his napkin to wipe tears from his eyes. "That's my boy. That's my boy."

Next to her, she could feel Declan relax by degrees as his father's mirth set the tone for the rest of the evening. It was a relief when after dessert everyone else took their leave and left them to their coffee.

"That went better than I expected," Declan commented with a relieved sigh after the last of their companions left the restaurant.

"Yes. It did." Gwen fidgeted with her napkin in her lap. It had gone better than she'd expected. Obviously people had seen what they wanted to. There'd be no threat to her security now. She'd passed this hurdle, she could pass whatever else came her way.

"We should go, too. I have an early flight to Christchurch tomorrow." He stood to pull out Gwen's chair when he suddenly halted.

"What?" Gwen looked up to see all colour flee his face. "Declan, what's wrong?"

"Nothing. Let's go." He grabbed her silver evening purse off the table and thrust it in her hands.

"Declan? Declan Knight?" A man's voice halted their progress through the restaurant.

With a muttered curse Declan put a restraining hand on her arm and turned to greet the man who hailed them. The familiarity of the other man's voice struck a cold chill down Gwen's spine. No, it couldn't be. Not Renata's father. Not here. Not now. Declan kept a hand at her back as they made their way through to Renata's parents' table.

"Declan! Gwen! Fancy seeing the two of you together. Please, take a seat." Renata's father smiled, gesturing to the two empty seats in their booth.

"Trevor. Dorothy." Declan nodded at them both. "It's a surprise to see you here in Auckland."

"Oh, we come once a year. Time to catch up with friends and visit Renata's grave—it would've been her birthday today, remember? Oh—" Renata's mother grabbed Declan's hand. "Is that a wedding ring I see? Trevor, look. They're married."

"M-married? You and Gwen?"

Gwen stood mute. She couldn't speak if she'd tried. She'd known these people since she was a teenager, had stood beside them at their only daughter's funeral. The air around them grew so thick you could cut it with a knife, and she began to regret the small portion of her dinner she'd managed to consume.

"Well, congratulations you two. Has it been long?" Trevor tried manfully to hide his surprise.

"Just over a month," Declan replied smoothly. "I'm sorry we can't stop with you, though. Maybe another time?"

"Yes, that would be lovely." Dorothy's enthusiasm appeared genuine and Gwen's heart sank. How on earth could they dream of attempting to fool these people? She didn't want to hurt them any more than she could bear another hurt herself. Dorothy stood up and wrapped her arms around Gwen with a tight hug. "We've missed you, honey. Both of you."

"I've missed you, too." Gwen's voice thickened with emotion. It had been crucifying to meet their gaze as, stricken with grief, they'd asked her why their daughter had to die. She'd failed them as much as she'd failed Renata that awful day.

"Don't be a stranger, promise? Now go on, get away with you. I bet you two can't wait to get home." Dorothy gave Gwen a gentle squeeze before releasing her.

Whether she said farewell or not Gwen couldn't

remember, all she knew was she had to get out of there. Away from the unspoken questions. The journey home was mercifully swift, and the minute Declan pushed open the door at the house Gwen raced forward on unsteady legs for the bathroom. Her stomach heaved until she could do no more. A cool washcloth wiped her face clean. Wiped away the tears that streaked her face. Wiped away the last of the dignity that she'd struggled to maintain.

"Oh, God. That was awful," she whispered, her voice shook like the last dry autumn leaves clinging to a branch.

"Yeah. It was."

Gwen pushed away from the toilet bowl and sank back on her heels. Declan grabbed a glass from the vanity, splashed cool tap water into it and handed it to her. Its velvet caress soothed as it slid down her tortured throat.

"Thanks. I'll be okay, now." She stood up and handed him the glass.

"Are you sure?"

"I have to be, don't I?" She stepped over to the basin and grabbed her toothbrush and paste. Her hands only trembled a little as she squeezed paste from the tube. Her heart hammered a little less frantically in her chest now. In the mirror she met Declan's eyes. "What about you? That can't have been easy."

"No, it wasn't. But it can't be undone. They expect to catch up with us at some time."

"We have to put them off. Wait until it's over then let them know with a letter."

"Is that what you really want to do?"

Gwen couldn't meet his cold stare any longer. Was that what she wanted? If the truth be told she really didn't know anymore. All she wanted was some guarantee that the pain would stop sometime soon. That the heartbreak would end. And that could only happen once he was out of her life for good. She lifted her eyes to meet his again. "Yes."

He didn't answer but somehow something in his eyes died a little at her response. With no more than a nod he turned and left the room.

Declan paced the floor of his room like a caged tiger. Each step on this crooked road brought new trials. It should have been easy—get married, stay married for six months, then get a divorce. But every minute of every day reminded him of the futility of loving someone who couldn't love him back. In some ways losing Renata had been easier than this. At least it was final. Learning to cope with her loss, learning to live with the grief, that had grown into something manageable. But this? This was sheer torture.

Declan ripped his tie from his neck and cast it across the room. Across the hall he heard Gwen's bedroom door gently close. Just a few metres, that's all it was, only a few steps and he could be across the hall and at her door, in her room—in her arms. It was as close as that, yet farther away than the dark side of the moon.

During the next few weeks they barely saw one another. To Gwen's relief, Declan was tied up in long, hard hours supervising the completion of the outstanding Cavaliere Developments contracts. Staggered over the next few months they'd free up his crews so that once the title to the Sellers building came through he'd be in a position to eventually bring everyone together to work on the ambitious project. The deadline to get the display apartment finished and ready to market was hellish, but

Gwen knew he'd get there. If there was one thing Declan Knight excelled at it was getting what he wanted.

While he worked flat out at the office and on various commissioned sites around New Zealand, Gwen laboured at home. She'd organised a contractor to complete installation of the shower in the bathroom while she finished the floor and walls. At his suggestion she'd also decided to convert the dressing room off the master bedroom into an en suite bathroom. That way there'd be even less chance of catching Declan in a state of undress.

Deep inside her body tightened as she unwillingly remembered the last time she'd seen him so. How his eyes had glittered as he'd looked up at her, how his powerful body had trembled beneath her touch—hers to command. Their lovemaking had been incendiary the first time, eight years ago—driven by grief and the desperate need to seek solace by losing themselves in one another—but the second... She sighed. That had been different altogether.

For the first time in years, Gwen had *wanted* to reach out to someone. To be a part of someone else on a scale she'd never dreamed could exist between herself and another person. The painful irony that it had been Declan wasn't lost on her. It seemed as though if she was going to make a mistake, she was destined to make it with him.

Gwen took a deep breath. She'd drawn on old reserves and shored up the walls around her heart— putting the past behind her again. To keep busy she worked hard, adding the finishing touches to the bathroom and putting toiletries and accessories back where they belonged. Her hand lingered on Declan's robe as she hung it up on the hook behind the door. A hint of his cologne wafted past to torment her senses. She pulled her hand back as if burned. God, she was such a weak fool.

Once everything was done she looked back upon the room. Sunlight refracted through the large stained-glass window set into the windowframe, sending jewel-like colours scattering over the polished wooden floor. The claw-footed bath had been professionally resurfaced and the new shower stall in the corner of the room looked as though it was meant to be there.

It was bittersweet success to have finished the main bathroom. Satisfying because she'd completed it on her own, yet disappointing for exactly the same reason. She brushed furiously at the tears that hovered in her eyes, as they seemed to do so often lately. Stop being so overemotional, Gwen growled at her reflection in the rimu-framed bathroom mirror. It was ridiculous to be weepy over having exactly what she wanted. By the time this ridiculous farce of a marriage was over, her house would be complete and, best of all, completely hers. That was all that mattered now. That and completing the terms of her contract with Cavaliere Developments.

Twelve

Gwen stood up from the chair and stretched her back to work out the kinks. She'd been at it for hours but finally she'd completed her check of the inventory of furnishings stored in the Sellers Hotel's gloomy basement. Sourcing other period furnishings to match would be a challenge, but where necessary she had a short list of craftsmen who could replicate many of the fixtures. A thrill of excitement surged through her. Her whole career she'd waited for an opportunity like this— a chance to showcase her talents and bring the beauty of yesteryear to functional life again.

Her planning stages for the job were complete. Soon the physical work, the part she loved the most, could begin in earnest. Her own team of experts awaited her confirmation so they could swarm over the showcase apartment ready to work their magic. The hotel itself had harked back to a time when ceilings were high, rooms were spacious and suites were plentiful. Previous renovations to increase room numbers over the years had been done as cost effectively as possible, in most cases simply partitioning rooms. This meant the reconstruction had been minimal, and Declan's crews worked in shifts around the clock to get the rebuild done. Before long the showcase apartment would be laid open to her ministrations. She couldn't wait.

Everything was on schedule. It should have delighted her to know that within two months she'd be a free woman. The bank had called this week to confirm the money Steve had stolen from her had been deposited back on her account this week. Her heart gave a little twist. That would mean that Declan's money was back in his control, too. Would he still insist their marriage spin out for the full six months now that they had their money? With the board's approval for the job he could raise any number of loans if he needed to. A shiver ran down her back.

She flicked a glance at her watch. Damn, she was running late. In keeping with their façade she'd arranged a birthday celebration at home for Declan. If she didn't hurry she wouldn't have everything ready on time.

The party was going well. They'd been extremely lucky with the weather, and despite the recent cold snap the day had dawned bright and clear. Guests spilled out through the French doors in the dining room and onto the deck. Conversations hummed all around, including many exclamations over Gwen's successful work on the house. If she hadn't been contracted to the Sellers job she'd probably have work coming out of her cars based on tonight alone.

She tried to relax the knot of tension in her stomach. *Nerves,* she told herself. Just nerves. It was the first party she'd hosted as Declan's wife and would, no doubt, be the last. It had to be perfect. Satisfied at last that everyone was well catered to, Gwen picked up a glass of chilled chardonnay and drifted outside to join their guests in enjoying the final strains of evening light before the crispness of the autumn night air could force them indoors.

Declan knew the minute Gwen came outside to join the crowd. He watched as she sank gracefully into one of the wicker chairs on the deck, the smile on her face as she greeted someone not quite reaching her eyes. Living together was hell on his senses, and he'd all but managed to convince himself that his feelings for her were under control, until he'd heard the news from his bank that the money Crenshaw had squirreled away overseas was now back where it belonged.

They didn't have to keep this up any longer. Life could revert to normal. He'd already pegged out the apartment he'd have for his own in the Sellers building. He could move back in with Mason until it was finished and get this over with even faster. The thought should've made him feel better, but it didn't.

He should've known better than to let his emotions take over. Emotions he'd controlled since the day his mother died and left him in charge of his younger brothers. Had he ever really let himself grieve for her? He couldn't remember. For so long he'd been the one to take charge. To make sure everyone's needs were met. It was easier to be busy than to think. Way easier. Now it was time to take charge again.

"Excuse me," he said to the guest he'd been talking

with. "I need to see my wife." He cut through the chatting throng of guests to catch up at Gwen's side just as his father sat next to her.

"So when are you two going to grace me with some grandchildren to spoil? Huh?" Tony Knight leaned forward to plant a kiss on each of Gwen's pale cheeks.

Pale? Yes, she was paler than normal. Declan made a mental note to talk to her about enlisting another contractor to help out here at the house. She pushed herself too hard. He'd known it for ages yet had done nothing about it. With her work at home and what she was already doing at the hotel she'd spread herself too thin—and it was his fault.

"I…" At his father's blustering comment Gwen seemed lost for words.

It was time he interceded. "Hey, Dad. We've only been married four months and you want us to have kids?"

Tony winked slowly at his son and gave him a gentle punch on the arm. "You enjoy your honeymoon, son. The hard work comes soon enough." Then with a hearty laugh at his own joke he wandered off.

"We're going to get a lot of that," Declan commented, watching his father looking more relaxed and happier than he'd seen him in years.

"Only for as long as we're married." Gwen's blunt reply left subtlety to the wind. It was obvious she couldn't wait to get out of the arrangement.

Declan looked at her assessingly. Up close the ravages of her hard work showed more plainly on her face. She looked tired and unhappy. The knowledge that he was responsible for all that twisted like a knife in his gut. He couldn't stand it any longer. There was only one thing he could do.

The honourable thing.

Finding Connor in the crowd was easy. His baby brother stood head and shoulders above most people. He rose from his chair and made a beeline for him.

"You okay, big bro'?" Connor passed him an icy-cold beer. "With a face like that you won't need to blow out your candles, you can just scare them away."

"Lay off, Connor," he growled in response.

"Ouch, testy!" Connor took a sip of his drink. "So, what gives? If I didn't know better I'd say you're having trouble with your beautiful wife."

"What do you mean, if you didn't know better?"

"Cut me some slack, Dec. I drew up the agreement, remember? You guys have a deal."

Yeah, they had a deal. But they'd irrevocably broken one of the conditions, and his life had been in the sewer since. "Maybe it's old age creeping up on me." Declan smiled with a rueful twist to his lips.

"Happens to the best of us, some sooner than others." Connor grinned back.

"While we're on the subject, what would happen if we rescind the agreement?" Declan pitched the question with as casual an air as he could muster.

Connor looked shocked. "Rescind it? You'd have to have a bloody good reason, Dec. The conditions of the trust fund are very specific. Whether you need it now or not, you don't just throw that kind of money down the drain. We are talking several million here."

Declan fixed his gaze on Gwen's face as she circulated among their guests. "Do it. Let it revert to Dad's trust."

"You know you only get one shot at this under Mum's terms. Are you absolutely sure that's what you want?"

"Yeah." Declan's voice hardened. "Never more so."

* * *

The last of the guests had left by nine and Gwen looked forward to putting herself to bed. Declan's voice halted her on her way to her room.

"Gwen? Can you come into the sitting room for a moment? I need to talk to you."

A cold prickle of apprehension caressed her neck. The last time he'd *needed* to talk to her he'd thrown their lovemaking straight back in her face.

"Can't it wait until tomorrow, Declan? I'm very tired."

He sighed and pushed a hand through his hair. "I know. Please, this won't take long."

Gwen followed him into the sitting room. As the evening had drawn in and their guests had filtered back indoors someone had lit the fire. The flames licked and danced their way merrily over the split logs, creating a soothing ambience. She avoided using this room as much as possible, the memories of when they'd first lit the fire too painful to dwell on.

Declan stood by the mantel, a deeply serious expression throwing the planes of his face into stark relief. He gestured to her to sit down. As she did, Gwen felt her heartbeat pick up a few notches. He took a bunch of papers from the top of the mantelpiece and held them in his hand. Was it her imagination or did she see the typed sheets shake? No, there it was again. Unease crept icily through her veins, freezing her in her seat.

"I thought it would be easy, you know?" Declan's onyx gaze sought hers. She felt trapped but nothing could induce her to move. She knew to the soles of her feet she had to hear what he needed to say. "Being married to you, in name only. Hell, I kidded myself I could do it, no matter what had happened between us.

No matter how much I despised both of us for what happened when Renata died." A cynical twist pulled briefly at his lips. "I was wrong."

He turned and held the papers towards the fire.

"What are you doing?" Gwen cried as a finger of flame caressed one corner before the paper turned black and began to burn.

"I'm destroying our agreement. You're free, Gwen."

"But you can't do that! What about your trust fund?" Gwen shot to her feet.

"The hell with the trust fund." He dropped the fiercely burning sheets into the fireplace and pulled the antique screen in front.

"Why?" She blinked furiously at the sudden tears that sprang to her eyes. Rejected again? How many ways could he hurt her? She thought she was stronger than this. After all, wasn't it what she wanted? All or nothing? Except he was giving her nothing and it cut into her like shards of a broken mirror. "Is it that now you've got your money back you don't need the fund? You don't need me?"

"Don't worry about your job. That's still safe, if you want it. And if you don't, I'll still honour the salary I was paying you until you get set up again."

"I don't care about the job, Declan. Why are you doing this?"

Declan turned and put both hands on the mantelpiece and dropped his head between his shoulders. "I can't do it anymore, Gwen. It's tearing me apart. I know what it's like living with losing someone you've loved. Trying to come to terms with it every day that you'll never see them, never hold them again. It killed me inside and now I'm doing it to you, too. You have your freedom. I'm moving out tonight."

Freedom? Moving out? What the hell was he on about? "That doesn't explain anything. Why are you pushing me away?" Her throat closed, thickened with emotion. Darn it, why couldn't she control the unsteadiness in her voice?

"I'm not pushing you, Gwen." He turned and faced her again. "Don't you understand, you're free of me. Connor will start proceedings on Monday."

If he'd ripped out her heart he couldn't have caused her more pain. With agonising clarity Gwen suddenly knew what she'd been fighting for years. She loved Declan Knight. She always had. Agreeing to marry someone like Steve had been denial of the truth, denial of the fact that she was worth more. Worth the love of a man who'd put her first before anything else, and she'd have to do everything in her power to make sure she held on to it—to him.

"No, you can't..We have a deal."

A log on the fire hissed loudly as sap bubbled from a crack in the wood.

"I've already given Connor my instructions."

"Then tell him to stop." Gwen bunched her hands into fists. Somehow she had to get through to Declan, to convince him to give her another chance.

"C'mon, Gwen. You know you don't want to be married to me. You're still in love with Steve Crenshaw. It was his name you cried in your sleep after we made love."

She'd hurt more than his male pride with what she'd done, and the knowledge gave her one tiny ember of hope. In that short speech he'd told her everything. The ember flared into something larger, giving her the courage and the impetus to press forward.

"That upset you?"

"Damn right it upset me."

Good, he was starting to look angry. Anything was better than the noble martyred expression he'd worn before. Anger she could deal with. Anger was real. Anger could be defused.

"Why?" she prodded.

"Any man would be insulted if the woman he'd just had sex with called him by another man's name."

"And you were insulted?"

"Insulted? No. I was devastated."

"Why were you devastated, Declan? Tell me." Gwen stepped towards him, and placed her hand against his chest. His heart beat like a crazy thing beneath her hand.

"It doesn't matter anymore."

"It was a mistake, what I said. If I could find any way to take it back I would. I'm sorry, Declan."

"Yeah, so am I. I'm sorry I ever thought this would work. Now, you're free, I'm free. We can go back to our lives."

She couldn't let it rest there. She had to draw every last stubborn word out of him, even if it was like pulling out rusted upholstery staples with a pair of chopsticks.

"Why did you want it to work between us? Tell me." Her voice was low, insistent. With a need born of desperation she had to hear his answer.

"Because I love you, Gwen. For all the good that does me." He pushed her hand away from his chest and went to walk away but Gwen grabbed hold of his arm.

"Don't you dare walk away from me now, Declan Knight."

Gwen butted up to him, chest to chest and poked a pointed finger at his arm. "Why didn't you ask me why I called Steve's name?"

"Oh, yeah, like that would've made good breakfast conversation. Sure." Sarcasm dripped like poisoned icicles from his mouth.

"I dreamed about him. A nightmare. If I called his name, it was in fear, not passion. All my passion is for you." Gwen emphasised each point with another stab of her finger.

"Is?"

"Yes. *Is*. I don't want to be married to you for six months—or a year! I want to be with you forever. And I've never been more frightened in my entire life." Gwen took his face in both hands. "Don't you dare tell me I have my *freedom*. I don't want it. I haven't been free since I agreed to marry you, because even though we married for all the wrong reasons, despite how we may have fooled ourselves how right they were, I never believed I could be worthy of the love of a man like you."

"But, Gwen…"

She placed a finger on his lips. "Hear me out, please. My father left my mother when I was six years old. I saw first-hand how loving someone so much scarred him so deeply he couldn't bear the sight of her, or me as a constant reminder of how she'd betrayed him. And you know, despite everything, she was never the same after that. She was a beautiful woman—still is. Any man would be proud to have her on his arm. But all that meant nothing when my father stopped loving her. She's spent every day since looking for a man who'll love her like that again."

Tears filled her eyes. She tried to blink them away, but still they came. "You know, when I was tiny, he would pull me on his lap and tell me I was his beautiful princess. His treasure. I felt like I owned the world when I was with him. When he found out I wasn't his child he just cast us away.

"Knowing how my mother's behaviour drove them apart, seeing her constant need for reassurance that she was beautiful, I swore I could make a marriage work without physical attraction but, God help me, I couldn't control that with you. Eight years ago, what we shared was the most overwhelming and most beautiful thing I'd ever experienced. But it was totally wrong. We reached for one another for all the wrong reasons and they destroyed any chance we had to build something special together.

"I tried to tell myself it didn't matter—that you didn't matter to me. But I got a second chance when Steve did what he did. It brought you back into my life, into my house. Into my heart. I love you, Declan, with all that I am. Don't tell me this is over."

"Over?" Declan wrapped his arms around his wife. "No, this isn't over. We've only just begun." He bent his head and tenderly caught her lips and it was as though he kissed her for the first time. Completely, honestly, with love.

He swept her into his arms and carried her down the hallway. "Your place or mine?" he asked with a devilish gleam in his eye.

Gwen laughed gently. "Oh, yours, please. I've coveted that bed from the day you moved in."

"We haven't finished decorating in here."

"I won't be looking at the walls, I promise you."

He lay her gently on the bed before stretching the full length of his body alongside hers and lifted one hand to stroke the outline of her face. Gwen watched as his eyes shimmered with emotion. When he finally bent his face

to hers she could barely hold back the sense of exulta-
tion that flooded her mind and her body. He was hers.

She threaded her hands into his hair and pulled him
harder to her, relishing the right she had to do so. His
lips fused with hers and his tongue swept gently into her
mouth, setting off tiny shocks of delight as he probed
the sensitive membrane of her inner lips.

She put her hands to work, divesting him of his shirt
and reaching for the buckle at his waist and loosening
his trousers so she could hold him in her hands. He
shuddered with pleasure at her touch, growling against
her mouth as she stroked the velvet length of him.

"You're wearing too many clothes," he groaned,
finally relinquishing her lips and pulling out of her reach.

"Why don't you do something about that then," she
answered softly with a smile that left him in no doubt
of her invitation.

Slowly, with infinite care, Declan removed each item
of clothing. She wanted to scream at him to hurry. To
just push her skirt up and take her like that. She wanted
him with a hunger that eclipsed anything she'd known
before. But still he took his time.

He trailed his fingers across her shoulders, then down
across her collarbone before pressing his heated lips to
her skin. She squirmed against the bedcovers, the
textured duvet cover igniting her bare skin where it
touched, making her press even harder against the
fabric. When Declan's tongue followed the trail of his
fingers down between her breasts and over her ribs,
ignoring the peaked swollen flesh of her breasts, she
couldn't hold back the moan of dissatisfaction.

"Touch me," she begged. "Please."

"Since you asked so nicely," he replied before letting

his fingers glide, feather soft across the creamy swell of her breast, first one then the other.

"More," she demanded, her voice thick with passion, thick with need for him.

She gasped and arched her back off the bed as he caught her nipple between his thumb and index finger, the pressure at first gentle then harder and tighter as he rolled the sensitive flesh between the pads. Then the other side as he manipulated both nipples. Wave after wave of pleasure rose within her and she pressed her eyes shut, focussed only on the sensation that radiated through her body. When the moist heat of his mouth replaced the fingers of one hand she toppled over the edge of reason and gave in to the pulse of pleasure that flooded her body, shuddering against his mouth, her fingers tangled in his hair.

When the final wave subsided she opened her eyes only to feel passion rise again with a new hunger as he traced the outline of her ribs with his tongue, then followed the fine line of indentation of her abdomen and lower to her belly button. His tongue dipped and swirled in the recess and a sharp dart of pleasure shot straight to her groin.

She had no voice left to protest as he gently pushed her legs apart and positioned himself between her thighs, his fingers sliding through the thatch of hair that protected her core. Her inner muscles clenched in anticipation as his warm breath whispered against her tender, swollen flesh. When his mouth closed over her and his tongue flicked over her sensitive bud she gave herself over to the beauty of the pleasure he gave her. Again her body climbed and soared, almost but not quite reaching the pinnacle of the pleasure his lips and tongue promised.

Her cry of protest split the air as he suddenly halted his ministrations and pulled away from her body. Through glazed eyes she watched as he slipped to the edge of the bed and removed the last of his clothing, kicking his pants across the room to land with a dull thud against the wall. Then he was back, his eyes blacker than darkest night as they held hers, his lips shining with her own moisture.

Gwen reached for his erection. His skin was taut, and hot—so hot. She guided him to her entrance, letting go only as he gently probed her before sliding full length within her body in one smooth motion. She lifted her hands to his shoulders, relishing the bunched power in his muscles as he held still, refusing to move.

Unable to stay still Gwen clenched her inner muscles again and pulled up to let her lips capture his. Then, thank God, he moved again, withdrawing from her body before plunging in again and again until finally she splintered into a million tiny particles of pleasure. Tears squeezed from her eyes at the beauty of this man—her husband—and the love he gave her. How could she ever have settled for anything less than this perfection, this rightness, this sense of belonging?

His climax, when it came, shook him in powerful waves and he collapsed against her, his body moulding to her shape as though they'd been carved from the same piece of clay. A smile of satisfaction and deep contentment played at her lips as she coasted her fingers up and down the length of his back, relishing the tiny tremors that shuddered through his body in aftershock.

He was hers. Finally, totally, hers.

Declan levered himself slightly up and rolled to one side, hooking an arm around her so she faced him, their bodies still joined, their hips and thighs still pressed together.

"Thank you," he murmured.

"You're very welcome. Thank *you*." She undulated her hips against his.

Declan laughed softly. "No, you silly goose. Not for that, although I'm certainly not complaining." He captured her lips again, drawing her lower lip between his teeth, letting them abrade the swollen flesh. "I mean thank you for loving me. This marriage of ours, the old one, I felt safe with that. It was something I thought I could control. I've needed to be in control for longer than I can remember, but you swept that all aside. You had me doing things, saying things that went totally against the grain.

"I understand how you felt about love. To much the same degree I saw how losing my mother altered my father from a happy family man to a driving workaholic who no longer had time for his sons. It was always the business before us. He couldn't bear to live without her, but neither could he abandon us totally.

"Sure I was there to pick up the slack with the others. But, man, we lost count of the number of nights we'd wake up and roll Dad into bed after he'd tied on a few at the local after work."

Declan looped one finger in a tendril of Gwen's hair and twirled it round and round, enjoying the silky soft feel of it against the coarseness of his skin.

"It used to make me so bloody angry to have all that responsibility. But I did it and I kept on doing it because I had to. One way or another, I learned to bury that piece of me that loved, exactly like he did. Despite how much I hated the way he behaved, the harder I tried to not be like him, the more like him I became and when Renata died the transformation was complete."

He drew in a deep breath and let it out in a rush. "I loved Renata, Gwen. Passionately. You know what she was like—so carefree, so outgoing. Completely outrageous. The complete opposite of me. It was like trying to carry a flame in your hand while a gale blew up from the south. When she died I blamed you for being there with her but more than that, I blamed myself because I wasn't and because I didn't try harder to talk her out of that climb. I could've prevented that fall—could've saved you both. I've lived with that every day of my life since."

"Declan, no," Gwen interrupted. "Don't crucify yourself like that. No one could've stopped Renata that day. She was determined. I only went with her because I was sure that my inexperience would hold her back a little. She knew I couldn't make that climb, that she'd have to button back. I begged her to let us go back down, and eventually she agreed. But by then it was too late."

Gwen pressed her lips to Declan's throat, taking comfort in the strength of his pulse against her lips. "We both loved her, Declan, but it's up to us now. We can't turn back the clock and undo time. We need to stop blaming ourselves for what happened, and move forward from today."

"Yeah, you're right. I can understand that now. You know, I think Renata and I would have gone through the rest of our lives chasing thrills but never quite making that final commitment." Declan tipped her chin up and pressed a kiss against her lips. "I never expected to fall in love again. Not like this. I can't believe how lucky I am to have you. I want to make a lifetime commitment to you. What we have is forever. Will you marry me, Gwen? Properly this time."

"Oh yes," she sighed against his lips. "That would make me the happiest woman in the world."

Declan ran his hand down the glorious, sinfully soft length of her back and pulled her body against his, feeling himself stir to life. He knew he would never have enough of her. His life couldn't be more complete. Tonight he'd been given the greatest gift of love. "Gwen, this has been the best birthday of my entire life. You're never going to top this one."

"Maybe not." Gwen smiled back. "But I'm going to spend the rest of my life trying."

* * * * *

Don't miss Mason Knight's story,
THE TYCOON'S HIDDEN HEIR,
available March 2007 from
Yvonne Lindsay and Silhouette Desire.

Happily ever after is just the beginning...

Turn the page for a sneak preview of
DANCING ON SUNDAY AFTERNOONS
by
Linda Cardillo.

*Harlequin Everlasting—Every great love
has a story to tell.* ™
*A brand-new line from Harlequin Books
launching this February!*

Prologue

Giulia D'Orazio
1983

I had two husbands—Paolo and Salvatore.

Salvatore and I were married for thirty-two years. I still live in the house he bought for us; I still sleep in our bed. All around me are the signs of our life together. My bedroom window looks out over the garden he planted. In the middle of the city, he coaxed tomatoes, peppers, zucchini—even grapes for his wine—out of the ground. On weekends, he used to drive up to his cousin's farm in Waterbury and bring back manure. In the winter, he wrapped the peach tree and the fig tree with rags and black rubber hoses against the cold, his massive, coarse hands gentling those trees as if they were his fragile-skinned babies. My neighbor, Dominic

Grazza, does that for me now. My boys have no time for the garden.

In the front of the house, Salvatore planted roses. The roses I take care of myself. They are giant, cream-colored, fragrant. In the afternoons, I like to sit out on the porch with my coffee, protected from the eyes of the neighborhood by that curtain of flowers.

Salvatore died in this house thirty-five years ago. In the last months, he lay on the sofa in the parlor so he could be in the middle of everything. Except for the two oldest boys, all the children were still at home and we ate together every evening. Salvatore could see the dining room table from the sofa, and he could hear everything that was said. "I'm not dead, yet," he told me. "I want to know what's going on."

When my first grandchild, Cara, was born, we brought her to him, and he held her on his chest, stroking her tiny head. Sometimes they fell asleep together.

Over on the radiator cover in the corner of the parlor is the portrait Salvatore and I had taken on our twenty-fifth anniversary. This brooch I'm wearing today, with the diamonds—I'm wearing it in the photograph also—Salvatore gave it to me that day. Upstairs on my dresser is a jewelry box filled with necklaces and bracelets and earrings. All from Salvatore.

I am surrounded by the things Salvatore gave me, or did for me. But, God forgive me, as I lie alone now in my bed, it is Paolo I remember.

Paolo left me nothing. Nothing, that is, that my family, especially my sisters, thought had any value. No house. No diamonds. Not even a photograph.

But after he was gone, and I could catch my breath from the pain, I knew that I still had something. In the middle of the night, I sat alone and held them in my hands, reading the words over and over until I heard his voice in my head. I had Paolo's letters.

* * * * *

Be sure to look for
DANCING ON SUNDAY AFTERNOONS
available January 30, 2007.
And look, too, for our other
Everlasting title available,
FALL FROM GRACE by Kristi Gold.

FALL FROM GRACE is a deeply emotional story
of what a long-term love really means.
As Jack and Anne Morgan discover,
marriage vows can be broken—
but they can be mended, too.
And the memories of their marriage
have an unexpected power
to bring back a love that never really left....

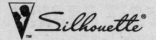

Romantic
SUSPENSE

Excitement, danger and passion guaranteed!

Same great authors and riveting editorial
you've come to know and love.

Look for our new name next month
as Silhouette Intimate Moments® becomes
Silhouette® Romantic Suspense.

Bestselling author
Marie Ferrarella
is back with a hot
new miniseries—
The Doctors Pulaski:
Medicine just got
more interesting....

Check out her
first title,
HER LAWMAN
ON CALL,
next month.

Look for it wherever
you buy books!

Visit Silhouette Books at www.eHarlequin.com

SIMRS0107

REQUEST YOUR FREE BOOKS!

2 FREE NOVELS PLUS 2 FREE GIFTS!

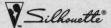

Passionate, Powerful, Provocative!

YES! Please send me 2 FREE Silhouette Desire® novels and my 2 FREE gifts. After receiving them, if I don't wish to receive any more books, I can return the shipping statement marked "cancel." If I don't cancel, I will receive 6 brand-new novels every month and be billed just $3.80 per book in the U.S., or $4.47 per book in Canada, plus 25¢ shipping and handling per book and applicable taxes, if any*. That's a savings of almost 15% off the cover price! I understand that accepting the 2 free books and gifts places me under no obligation to buy anything. I can always return a shipment and cancel at any time. Even if I never buy another book from Silhouette, the two free books and gifts are mine to keep forever.

225 SDN EEXJ 326 SDN EEXU

Name	(PLEASE PRINT)	
Address		Apt.
City	State/Prov.	Zip/Postal Code

Signature (if under 18, a parent or guardian must sign)

Mail to Silhouette Reader Service™:

IN U.S.A.
P.O. Box 1867
Buffalo, NY
14240-1867

IN CANADA
P.O. Box 609
Fort Erie, Ontario
L2A 5X3

Not valid to current Silhouette Desire subscribers.

Want to try two free books from another line?
Call 1-800-873-8635 or visit www.morefreebooks.com.

* Terms and prices subject to change without notice. NY residents add applicable sales tax. Canadian residents will be charged applicable provincial taxes and GST. This offer is limited to one order per household. All orders subject to approval. Credit or debit balances in a customer's account(s) may be offset by any other outstanding balance owed by or to the customer. Please allow 4 to 6 weeks for delivery.

SDES06

HARLEQUIN®

Super Romance®

Is it really possible to find true love
when you're single...with kids?

Introducing an exciting new five-book miniseries,

SINGLES...WITH KIDS

When Margo almost loses her bistro...and custody of
her children...she realizes a real family is about more
than owning a pretty house and being a perfect mother.
And then there's the new man in her life, Robert...
Like the other single parents in her support group, she
has to make sure he wants the whole package.

Starting in February 2007 with

LOVE AND THE SINGLE MOM

by C.J. Carmichael

(Harlequin Superromance #1398)

ALSO WATCH FOR:

THE SISTER SWITCH Pamela Ford (#1404, on sale March 2007)
ALL-AMERICAN FATHER Anna DeStefano (#1410, on sale April 2007)
THE BEST-KEPT SECRET Melinda Curtis (#1416, on sale May 2007)
BLAME IT ON THE DOG Amy Frazier (#1422, on sale June 2007)

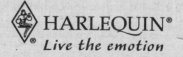

HARLEQUIN®
Live the emotion

www.eHarlequin.com   HSRLSM0207

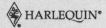

EVERLASTING LOVE™

Every great love has a story to tell™

Save $1.⁰⁰ off

the purchase of any Harlequin Everlasting Love novel

Coupon valid from January 1, 2007 until April 30, 2007.

Valid at retail outlets in the U.S. only. Limit one coupon per customer.

RETAILER: Harlequin Enterprises Limited will pay the face value of this coupon plus 8¢ if submitted by the customer for this product only. Any other use constitutes fraud. Coupon is nonassignable. Void if taxed, prohibited or restricted by law. Consumer must pay any government taxes. Void if copied. For reimbursement submit coupons and proof of sales directly to: Harlequin Enterprises Ltd., P.O. Box 880478, El Paso, TX 88588-0478, U.S.A. Cash value 1/100¢. Valid in the U.S. only. ® is a trademark of Harlequin Enterprises Ltd. Trademarks marked with ® are registered in the United States and/or other countries.

5 65373 00076 2   (8100) 0 11302

HEUSCPN0407

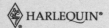

EVERLASTING LOVE™

Every great love has a story to tell ™

Save $1.⁰⁰ off

the purchase of
any Harlequin
Everlasting Love novel

Coupon valid from January 1, 2007
until April 30, 2007.

Valid at retail outlets in Canada only.
Limit one coupon per customer.

RETAILER: Harlequin Enterprises Limited will pay the face value of this coupon plus 10.25¢ if submitted by the customer for this product only. Any other use constitutes fraud. Coupon is nonassignable. Void if taxed, prohibited or restricted by law. Consumer must pay any government taxes. Void if copied. Nielsen Clearing House customers submit coupons and proof of sales to: Harlequin Enterprises Ltd. P.O. Box 3000, Saint John, N.B. E2L 4L3. Non–NCH retailer—for reimbursement submit coupons and proof of sales directly to: Harlequin Enterprises Ltd., Retail Marketing Department, 225 Duncan Mill Rd., Don Mills, Ontario M3B 3K9, Canada. Valid in Canada only. ® is a trademark of Harlequin Enterprises Ltd. Trademarks marked with ® are registered in the United States and/or other countries.

52607370

HECDNCPN0407

What a month!

In February watch for

Rancher and Protector
Part of the Western Weddings miniseries
BY JUDY CHRISTENBERRY

The Boss's Pregnancy Proposal
BY RAYE MORGAN

Also in February, expect
MORE of what you love
as the Harlequin Romance line
increases to six titles per month.

Silhouette®

Desire

Don't miss the first book
in THE ROYALS trilogy:

THE FORBIDDEN PRINCESS
(SD #1780)

by national bestselling author
DAY LECLAIRE

Moments before her loveless royal wedding,
Princess Alyssa was kidnapped by a mysterious man
who'd do anything to stop the ceremony. Even if that
meant marrying the forbidden princess himself!

On sale February 2007 from Silhouette Desire!

THE ROYALS
Stories of scandals and secrets
amidst the most powerful palaces.

Make sure to read the other titles in the series:
THE PRINCE'S MISTRESS
On sale March 2007

THE ROYAL WEDDING NIGHT
On sale April 2007

*Available wherever books are sold, including most
bookstores, supermarkets, discount stores and drugstores.*

Visit Silhouette Books at www.eHarlequin.com   SDTFP0207